Adapted by Elizabeth Rudnick

Based on a screenplay by Alex Ross Perry and Allison Schroeder

Story by Alex Ross Perry

Based on characters created by A. A. Milne and E. H. Shepard

LOS ANGELES • NEW YORK

For information address Disney Press, 1200 Grand Central Avenue, Glendale, California 91201.

Winnie the Pooh is based on the "Winnie the Pooh" works by A. A. Milne and E. H. Shepard.

Printed in the United States of America
First Paperback Edition, July 2018
1 3 5 7 9 10 8 6 4 2
FAC-020093-18138

Library of Congress Control Number: 2017959507

ISBN 978-1-368-02590-4

disneybooks.com
http://movies.disney.com/christopher-robin

THIS LABEL APPLIES TO TEXT STOCK

To my very own Jameson Milne, who reminds me every day of the power that lies in imagination

AUTHOR'S NOTE

As a child, I spent many afternoons lost in the Hundred-Acre Wood, caught up in adventures with a silly old bear named Pooh and his best friend, Christopher Robin. The world of the wood was as real to me as my own backyard. I could picture Pooh's home, with its large armoire full of honey pots, and felt as though I, myself, had knocked on Piglet's door on many occasions. I loved Eeyore, with his droopy eyes and pessimistic view on life (though at the time, I had no idea what *pessimistic* meant). I just thought it was rather funny that the donkey could never see how much he was loved or how great things were (a lesson I remind myself of often in my older age) and wanted a hug from Kanga and to bounce along with Roo and Tigger.

Rabbit and Owl, with their more serious natures and understanding of the larger world, always intimidated me to a degree but became the characters I saw most in the adult figures in my life. The Hundred-Acre Wood was a wonderful place to spend my time—and generations of children before and after me have also lost themselves among the woods and its hodgepodge of animals. What child hasn't, at some point or another, believed in that innocent, wholehearted way that the stuffed animals they loved the most could come to life and be their companions on adventures, that they could provide comfort when faced with the inevitable sad or frightening moments of life.

Pooh was that hope come true—and even now, I believe in him and what he represented. I believe in the silly old bear who could, in his simple way, always find the silver lining and bring the world to right when it got knocked off-kilter. As Pooh himself so wisely said, "Life is a journey to be experienced, not a problem to be solved." Enjoy the adventure!

—E. Rudnick

"You can't stay in your corner of the forest waiting for others to come to you. You have to go to them sometimes."

—A. A. Milne

PROLOGUE

IN WHICH CHRISTOPHER ROBIN
AND POOH COME TO AN ENCHANTED PLACE
AND WE LEAVE THEM THERE

IT was, as it most usually was, a beautiful day in the Hundred-Acre Wood. The sky was blue, unblemished by clouds. The air was sweet, touched by the hint of honey that wafted from a familiar bear's pot, and a gentle breeze kissed the cheeks of the friends who had gathered around a picnic table. But while the setting was idyllic and lent itself to happy thoughts, the expressions on the faces of the friends were rather, well, sad.

Looking around the table, Winnie the Pooh tried to ignore the rumbling, grumbling sound coming from his tummy. He wasn't positive, but he had a feeling that now was not the time to mention he was hungry, even if they *were* at a picnic table—which, in his experience, was usually a place people picnicked. And picnics *usually* involved food. His tummy grumbled again.

"We all know why we're here."

Rabbit's serious voice brought a quick stop to thoughts of food. Pooh looked over and watched as Rabbit walked to the head of the picnic table. "I have asked my friend Eeyore"–he paused and nodded in the direction of the grey donkey, whose head was hanging down, as usual–"I have asked him to propose a rissolution."

Pooh cocked his head. *Rissolution?* He did not like when Rabbit used such big words. He opened his mouth to ask what a rissolution was, but before he could, Eeyore lumbered over to stand by Rabbit. He placed a piece of paper in the middle of the table and then proceeded to straighten it out–for a very long time. Finally, he cleared his throat and began to read: " 'Christopher Robin is going,' " he said, his voice slow and deep and, as usual, devoid of any happiness. " 'At least, I think he is. Where? Nobody knows. But he is going.' " Eeyore paused and his heavy brows furrowed as he looked over the words on the page. "I mean, 'he goes,' " he corrected himself. Then he went on. " 'Do we care? We do. Very much. Anyhow, we send our love. The end.' "

The sullen donkey stopped speaking and slowly lifted his head from the paper. The other animals were silent. Pooh was looking beyond him at the large banner they had hung above the picnic table. The words FAIRWELL CHRISTOPHER ROBEM were written across it—not quite straight—in a mishmash of colors. Eeyore let out a long, slow sigh. "If anyone wants to clap," he said finally, with little enthusiasm in his voice, "now is the time to do it."

As if on cue, Christopher Robin himself walked into the clearing.

"That's a lovely poem, Eeyore," he said in a kind voice. The seven-year-old had been hanging back at the edge of the clearing until Eeyore had finished. Now he brushed back his auburn bangs, which had grown long and shaggy over the summer months, and looked around at all his friends. He felt a lump in his throat. He loved the odd collection of animals more than anything in the world. He loved sweet, innocent Piglet, with his squeaky voice and fear of, well, everything. There was

Kanga and her joey, Roo, and Tigger, who, even during this somber occasion, couldn't stop moving. Owl and Rabbit had remained serious the entire time, while Eeyore had managed to make the going-away poem sound even sadder than it was supposed to be.

And of course, there was his best friend, Winnie the Pooh. He was going to miss them all so much. They had spent so many long days together, playing in the woods behind his family's house. Without them around, the summer would have been painfully slow—and painfully lonely. Mother and Father were not exactly *fun* playmates.

Knowing that the others were looking at him intently, eager to see if he liked his banner and poem, Christopher tried hard to smile. But he could tell that the others knew he was sad. Especially Pooh.

"It's just too bad it's over," the bear said, pulling his red shirt down over his belly. "I would have liked it to go for a while longer."

With a nod of agreement, Christopher Robin walked over to the picnic table. His shirt and shorts, which had fit at the beginning of the summer, were now too small—and he found himself pulling them down in a similar fashion to how Pooh tugged on his clothes. (Although Christopher knew that Pooh's reason for a tight shirt wasn't so much growing *up* as growing rounder from the abundant honey he ate.)

Jumping up onto the picnic table so he was closer in height to Christopher Robin, Piglet approached the boy. Even now, after countless hours of playing and adventuring together, the small pig seemed nervous. Christopher Robin tried not to smile as Piglet, whose expression was far too big and serious for such a tiny creature, held out a small bag. "I m-made you this sack of Hundred-Acre Wood haycorns," he stammered. "They are my very f-f-favorite snack. Wherever you may go, they will remind you of the Hundred-Acre Wood."

Christopher Robin took the haycorns solemnly. "Thank you, Piglet," he said. The little creature nodded but didn't take his eyes off the sack of haycorns. "Would you like one?" Christopher added, noting the hungry way Piglet was eying the treats. To his credit,

Piglet shook his head. But his eyes stayed fixated on the bag. "Well, I don't think I'll need any help remembering, but I shall treasure them always," Christopher finally said, giving Piglet another sincere thank-you. He was trying desperately to stay happy, but seeing how sad his friends were and the trouble they had gone to to give him a farewell picnic just made Christopher even sadder than he had been when he had woken that morning.

The minutes leading up to when he had entered the wood that day had been utterly miserable. His mother had insisted he pack before he could play. Then she had told him to clean out the nursery and put his "baby" toys away, as he wouldn't need them now that he was a big boy attending big-boy boarding school. Despite a lengthy, and in his mind well-argued protest about the importance of keeping things as reminders, Mother wouldn't change her mind. So that had meant more time inside, sorting and putting things in storage. He hadn't even been able to enjoy his last lunch, even though it was his favorite—a peanut butter, banana, and honey sandwich—because Father had arrived with the car right in the middle and had started packing up all their luggage. There had been one brief moment when Christopher was sure they were going to leave before he could escape to the woods, but then, thankfully, Father had been distracted, pulled away to fix a broken pipe. Christopher had taken his chance and slipped away.

Arriving in the wood, he had hoped to get a break from the sadness he felt; but instead he found himself saying good-bye and feeling all the weepier by the moment.

Suddenly, the air was knocked from his lungs as Tigger threw his arms around Christopher and squished his face right up against the boy's. "I'm gonna miss ya, I am!" he said, bouncing up and down on his tail as he squeezed Christopher tight.

Christopher couldn't help himself—he let out a laugh. Tigger was always good for a laugh. And he provided Christopher with the distraction he greatly needed. "I'll miss you, too, Tigger," Christopher said. Then he turned to the others, determined to make the best of the rest of the picnic. "Now, c'mon, everyone! We still have pudding!"

* * *

The rest of the afternoon sped by in a flurry of pudding, playing, and feasting. As the sun sank lower and the woods grew darker, Christopher Robin's friends began to fall asleep, one by one, until soon the only two left awake were Christopher and Pooh. The others lay on or around the picnic table, peacefully slumbering. Well, most of them were peacefully slumbering. Even in his sleep, Tigger's feet and tail were in constant motion.

Pooh's nose was buried in a pot of honey. Around him, already emptied of their contents, were eight other pots. Most were tipped over, their insides honey free, and even their outsides licked completely clean. Pooh felt a party was not a party without honey—lots and lots of honey. And he would never let any of the sweet goodness go to waste.

"Come on, Pooh!"

Christopher's voice startled the bear and he pulled

his nose free from the pot. Christopher Robin was on his feet, standing by the edge of the clearing. Pooh got to his own feet and scampered—or rather waddled as fast as he could—over to his friend. "Where are we going, Christopher Robin?" he asked.

In the light of the setting sun, the little boy's hair seemed redder than usual, and in the wake of the excitement from the day, his cheeks looked flushed, while his freckles stood out. His yellow shirt, which had been clean when he'd arrived in the wood, was now stained from pudding and grass and various other party fun. Even the shirt's stiff white collar was sagging. Despite the long day, Christopher's brown eyes were shining and bright. "Nowhere," he said finally, answering Pooh.

"One of my favorite places," Pooh replied happily. Reaching up his paw, he waited for Christopher Robin to take it. The friends then turned and headed deeper into the woods together.

They walked in silence for a while, each happy to just be with the other. As they went, they recounted many of the adventures they had been on, often passing sights that triggered fond memories. They saw the tree where Pooh had tried to trick some honey bees by pretending to be a rain cloud only to end up landing—along with Christopher Robin—in a mudhole. They walked by Rabbit's house, where Pooh had gotten stuck, and then meandered under Owl's old home, which had once been blown down in a storm. Finally, they arrived in the large meadow hidden deep within the Hundred-Acre Wood. The sun was hovering over the horizon, turning the green grass gold.

As the two friends crossed through the meadow and toward Pooh Sticks Bridge, Christopher Robin looked down at his friend and asked, "What do you like doing best in the world, Pooh?"

"Well, what I like best . . ." He stopped and thought for a moment, tapping a finger against his chin. He furrowed his brow and made thinking noises. Arriving at an answer, he began again. "Well, what I like best is me and Piglet going to see you and you saying, 'What about a little Something?' And me saying, 'Well, I shouldn't mind a little Something.' And it being a hummy sort of day outside." Pooh looked up, proud of his answer.

Christopher Robin nodded but didn't say anything else until they arrived at Pooh Sticks Bridge. Peering over the edge of the bridge into the water below, he gazed at his reflection. He certainly didn't *look* any older than he had at the beginning of the summer. But his mother kept telling him he was a big boy now and that he had to act like one. He wasn't sure what that exactly meant. But he didn't think he liked it.

"What I like doing best is Nothing," he said finally.

Pooh cocked his head. "How do you do Nothing?" he asked, confused.

"It's when people call out, 'What are you going to do, Christopher Robin?' And you say, 'Oh, nothing,' and then you go and do it," he answered as though that were the most obvious answer in the whole world.

Pooh's eyes grew wide as understanding dawned. "Ah, yes!" he cried. "Doing Nothing often leads to the very best Something," he said.

Delighted that they understood one another's favorite things, the pair moved on. While he hadn't intended to, Christopher realized he was taking a farewell tour of his favorite spots in the Hundred-Acre Wood. The meadow, Pooh Sticks Bridge, the woods themselves—they all held such precious memories of the many adventures he had been on with his best friend. But none of them were as special to him as the Enchanted Place—the spot they finally arrived at just as the last rays of the sun snuck out over the horizon.

Below them, a valley stretched, its bottom already dark in the early evening. Looking out, Christopher felt his stomach drop as deep as the valley floor. He could walk all he wanted, but there was no denying what was to come. He let out a sigh that was sadder and longer than even Eeyore's saddest and longest sigh. "Pooh?" he said, turning to his friend. "I'm not going to do Nothing anymore."

The words struck Pooh like a slap to the face. "Never again?" he said in disbelief.

Christopher Robin shook his head. "Well, they don't

let you at boarding school. They—" As he spoke, he started to sit down. He let out a yelp.

"Haycorns hurt?" Pooh asked, assuming Christopher's response was to a loose haycorn that his backside had accidentally landed on.

Christopher Robin reached into the back pocket of his shorts, pulling out the bag of haycorns Piglet had given him. "Only when you sit on them," he said with a wry smile.

"I'll have to remember that," Pooh said, nodding at Christopher's wisdom. Looking over, Pooh saw that his friend's face was sad. He wondered if it had anything to do with the bored-ing school he had mentioned. Pooh had never heard of a bored-ing school before. Christopher had mentioned *school*, but that was a fun place where someone read you stories and you got to play with new toys and be with your friends. Bored-ing school didn't sound as fun. From the sound of Christopher's voice, it actually seemed like a very *un*-fun place. Pooh didn't like to think of his friend stuck in a place that wasn't fun or nice.

Just then, Christopher let out a sigh that seemed too big for such a small boy. "Pooh," he said softly, his gaze trained on the meadow in front of him. "When I'm off not doing Nothing, will you come up here sometimes?"

Pooh cocked his head. "Just me?" he asked. "Where will you be?"

"I'll be right here," Christopher answered. Lifting his hand, he tapped Pooh's "Thinking Spot"—the side of his head—with his finger.

That made sense to Pooh, and he nodded. Christopher was always in his Thinking Spot. That was where best friends were supposed to be—usually. "But what should happen if you forget about me?" Pooh asked, the thought hitting him hard. He felt sick suddenly, like when he discovered he had run out of honey. Or when he ate too much honey at once.

Christopher reached over and put his arm around Pooh's shoulder. "I won't ever forget you, Pooh," he said softly. "I promise. Not even when I'm a hundred."

Pooh frowned in concentration as he tried to calculate how old he would be when Christopher Robin was that old. His frown grew deeper and deeper until, finally, he realized he couldn't figure it out himself and just asked.

"Ninety-nine," Christopher replied, smiling.

Slowly, the boy got to his feet. Beside him, Pooh did the same. The sun had long since set, and while he had done his best to avoid it, he couldn't delay the inevitable. It was time for him to leave the Hundred-Acre Wood. His mother and father had made it clear—it was time to grow up. But as he looked around the place that had provided him with adventure and friends, he couldn't help wondering why growing up meant saying good-bye to the things he loved most. . . .

* * *

Christopher tugged at the starched white collar around his neck. It felt like it was choking him. Everything about his new school uniform felt like it was choking him, actually. The awful-looking thing, with its pressed pants and stiff jacket, complete with big ugly round buttons, had been waiting for him on his bed when he had arrived home the night before from his final trip to the Hundred-Acre Wood, along with the instruction to try it on to ensure the fit. An empty suitcase had been sitting next to the uniform with yet more instructions. These read simply: PACK.

While he had hoped that staying in the woods until nightfall would save him from the final round of packing, he had been wrong. Christopher had arrived home to a hasty dinner and was then sent to bed with a warning that they would be leaving early the next morning, and that his room better be emptied and his bags fully packed by then. Reaching his room, he hadn't had the heart or the energy to pack that night, instead falling into bed and burying his head in the pillow. Flopping over, he had seen a shooting star in the sky through his window and made a desperate wish that the morning would bring a change in his parents' hearts.

But sadly, that had not been the case. Instead of rising to the hoped-for news that he was no longer going to boarding school, he had been awakened by his mother's frantic shouts for him to hurry. He could hear his parents as they moved about the house below, checking to be sure that they had gotten everything they would need. It was unclear when they would be back next. Mr. Robin's job was growing increasingly more demanding, and with Christopher off at boarding school, the house could very well go empty until the following summer—if Christopher was that lucky.

"Christopher! Son! Let's go!"

Christopher's shoulders tensed at his father's voice. It was rare for the man to talk to him directly, leaving that up to Mrs. Robin for the most part. But ever since they had informed him that he would be going to boarding school, Christopher had seen a change in how his father treated him. It was almost like he no longer thought of Christopher as a baby (babies being the wife's domain, in Mr. Robin's opinion) but rather as a grown-up. He had even, on occasion, tried to engage Christopher in conversations, telling him about things that went on at his job or what had happened on the train ride to the country that particular visit. There was a part of Christopher that thought it was nice to have his father's attention for once.

But there was another part of him that thought it was strange and uncomfortable. He had, in all honesty, grown used to being somewhat ignored by his father—especially when they were at the country house. That was part of what had sent him to the Hundred-Acre Wood in the first place. The house had always felt confining when his father was there for the weekends, and he had looked for a place to escape, where he could make noise and have some fun without fear of his father getting upset.

"Christopher!"

His father's voice called out again, less comforting this time. Grabbing the suitcase off his bed, Christopher took one last look around his room. He said a silent good-bye to the toys on the shelves of the worn bookcase and a farewell to the pictures on the wall. He nodded to the collection of stuffed animals on the single chair in one corner, his eyes lingering on the stuffed bear with the red shirt. Then he left the room, shutting the door behind him.

Downstairs, the front door to the house was open, revealing a car sitting in the driveway. His father and mother stood beside it. While mere inches from each other, they seemed miles apart. Their eyes were gazing in opposite directions: Mr. Robin's were glued to the paper in his hand; Mrs. Robin's were raised up, staring at the fluffy white clouds as they drifted through the blue sky. But upon hearing their son's footsteps, their gazes swiftly swung toward him.

"Do you have everything?" Mrs. Robin asked as her husband took the suitcase from Christopher's hand and placed it in the boot of the car.

Christopher shrugged.

"Then we're off," Mr. Robin said, sliding into the back seat and gesturing for the rest of his family to do the same. Catching sight of his son's sad expression, he reached over and ruffled Christopher's hair. "Don't worry, Son," he said, the reassuring words sounding odd coming from the large man's stern face. "Boarding school will be a grand adventure, I promise you."

As the car began to move down the long driveway, Christopher didn't dare speak. Grand adventure? Boarding school was not going to be a grand adventure. Grand adventures were running through the Hundred-Acre Wood. Grand adventures were laying traps for the Heffalump. Grand adventures were scaling trees for honey. But as their country house faded from view, Christopher knew there was no use trying to tell his father any of that. He was going off to boarding school, and leaving his friends and adventures behind. Possibly forever.

* * *

Christopher stared down at the blank page in front of him. He was supposed to be filling it with numbers, doing arithmetic. But he found himself doodling pictures of Pooh instead.

He had been at boarding school for exactly twenty-one

days, four hours, and—he risked being caught taking a glance at the large clock that hung above the blackboard—four minutes. And each one of those days, hours, and minutes had been unbearable. Every morning the students were awakened at 7:00 a.m. on the dot and expected down in the large dining hall by 7:30 for what usually consisted of tasteless porridge and tea. The teachers sat on a platform above the students, their plates heaped with things that actually smelled delicious—waffles, bacon, fresh cream, and sweet fruit. This daily ritual only served to make their own food seem that much blander in comparison.

Then it was off to classes that lasted through the afternoon. Long, dull classes held in lifeless rooms. Large windows offered a glimpse of the beautiful manicured grounds that surrounded the school, but the only time Christopher got to actually enjoy them was during their recreation period. Unlike the other classes that seemed endless, the recreation class was short and typically only allowed for a few laps around one of the large fields before the boys were sent back inside.

His father's promise that school would be an adventure was proving, as Christopher had suspected, to be woefully wrong. When they had first pulled onto the grounds and he had caught sight of a handful of young boys such as himself, he had a brief flare of hope that maybe his father would be right. The boys all seemed about his age, and most wore the same dazed expression he knew covered his own face. But his hope had been short-lived. Moving into the room he shared with two other boys, Christopher had quickly discovered that most of the boys who were students at the prestigious boarding school were dull and lifeless, like the school itself. When he had pulled out a few of his childhood books to put on the shelf above his bed, his roommates had immediately begun to tease him, calling him "baby" and asking if he "needed a hug from his mommy." The books were hastily removed from the shelf and crammed under his bed, along with the few stuffed animals he had brought.

Since then, the teasing had only grown worse. While Christopher had spent much of his first seven years at his family's country home and had been tutored by kind governesses, the boys he now called his classmates had grown up being groomed to attend Grayford Prep. They were mean and cruel and, Christopher thought in his angrier moments, not at all the type who would be invited into the Hundred-Acre Wood.

He had tried his best to stay positive and find the bright side, just like Pooh would have done. But with each passing day, it was growing harder and harder. He wanted nothing more than to go back and see his friends and tell them how horrible it was being stuck behind the large wrought iron gates of the school. But he couldn't. Instead, he had learned to just keep his nose in his books, try to forget about the Hundred-Acre Wood, and not bring too much attention to himself. If he did that, he had discovered, he was able to go pretty much unnoticed.

Unfortunately, it didn't always work.

Sometimes, he just needed to see Pooh again. So, sometimes, he drew.

"Am I boring you, Mr. Robin?"

The teacher's voice, dangerously close, startled Christopher, and he looked up from the paper in front of him. He swallowed. The teacher was standing over him, a stern look on her face. In her hand she held a long ruler. She began to hit it against her other hand, the sound loud in the now silent room. Then, with a *whack*, she slammed the ruler down on the paper, the long rod landing right on the largest image of Pooh. The bear was leaning up against a tree, his hand in a honey pot, with a look of concentration on his gentle face.

"I suggest you open your textbook, Mr. Robin, and follow along," the teacher said, doing it for him. The sudden movement sent the drawing floating to the floor. Tapping one of the math problems, the teacher raised an eyebrow and then, turning, headed back to the front of the room to resume her lecturing.

As she walked away, Christopher tried to reach down and rescue the picture. But before his fingers could grasp it, the student across from him snatched it up. He looked down at the picture and sneered. "Nice bear, baby," he hissed, just loud enough for Christopher to hear. Then, with a look of pure evil pleasure, he crumpled up the drawing.

Christopher turned his face, hoping the bully wouldn't see the tears that threatened to spill down his cheeks. He knew it was only a drawing, but it was a drawing of Pooh. He wondered, as he looked out the window, what the silly old bear would think of all this. Pooh had never met anyone he didn't like—well, except for maybe a Heffalump, though he had never actually met or seen a Heffalump. Christopher smiled. The bear would probably end up liking the Heffalump. That was just the way he was. But even Pooh would probably not have liked the boys Christopher now found himself living with.

Not for the first time, Christopher wished he could just go find his friend and leave this place for good. But as the teacher continued to teach that day's math lesson, Christopher realized with a start that it was a foolish wish. He had not wanted to admit it, but he had known since the day he arrived that that part of his life was over. He was, as his father had said when he dropped him off, a "young man" now. It was his job to learn so that one day he could get a job and provide for his own family. Adventures in the woods and fun with his friends were a part of his childhood. If he wanted to ever fit in at Grayford Prep, he was going to have to put thoughts of Pooh and the Hundred-Acre Wood under his bed along with the rest of his toys.

I have to grow up, Christopher thought, bringing pencil to paper and beginning to copy down the math problem on the blackboard. As he wrote, he couldn't help glancing over at the crumpled drawing of Pooh now lying beneath the feet of the bully. Already the pencil marks were fading, covered over by the scuff marks made by the other boy's shoes. By the end of class, the image, along with Christopher's hopes for returning to the Hundred-Acre Wood, had all but faded completely away.

"Promise me you'll never forget me because if I thought you would, I'd never leave."

—A. A. Milne

CHAPTER ONE

TWENTY-SOME YEARS LATER...

The city of London was bustling. Men and women rushed along sidewalks lined with shops. Great hulking buildings were being raised stone by stone to make more room for the growing population. Factories on the outskirts of the city belched smoke into the air, turning the sky a hazy blue and keeping the sun's rays from reaching the cold, damp ground. Down on the streets, cars competed for space with one another, the narrow lanes not large enough for the behemoth vehicles that now made their way through the city. A young boy stood on one corner, holding up a paper and shouting the day's headlines for all to hear.

Rushing past, Christopher took no notice of the boy or the noise or the hundreds of people around him. His eyes were glued to the papers he held clutched in one hand. A briefcase dangled from his other hand, swinging back and forth in an almost happy manner at odds with the serious expression on its owner's face

Christopher, no longer a boy, looked tired. The dark brown coat he wore over his tweed suit hung on his thin frame, and there were bags under his eyes. His auburn hair, once thick and prone to flopping in front of his face, was cut short and shot through with hints of grey. As he ducked and weaved along the sidewalk, he seemed lost in his own sad, lonely world. A large black umbrella was tucked under the handle of the briefcase, and he wore a hat, prepared for rain despite the cloudless sky above. If nothing else, Christopher Robin liked to be prepared for anything.

Reaching his destination, he paused only long enough to look up at the large building. The facade of Winslow Luggage's headquarters was impressive, even to someone as serious as Christopher had come to be. Huge columns lined the front. Above them resided the company's logo, which was chiseled into the marble. A revolving door at the top of the steps leading into the building was in constant motion as people arrived and departed from Winslow.

With a quick glance at his watch to ensure he was still on time, Christopher jogged up the stairs and passed through the door. Inside the structure was just as grand as the outside. But this time Christopher took no notice of it whatsoever. Instead, he caught sight of his secretary standing by the bank of elevators and made a beeline toward her.

"Good morning, Mr. Robin," Katherine Dane said, holding her notepad at the ready.

Christopher gave her the briefest of nods. "Good morning, Ms. Dane," he answered, pushing past her and through the elevator doors that had just opened.

"Did you have a pleasant—"

His secretary didn't have a chance to finish. "I'd like them to reconsider the brass fittings," Christopher went on, ignoring Ms. Dane's attempt at human interaction. "On the chestnut wardrobes. Try nickel-plated fittings—"

"—evening?" Katherine finished anyway. She had been working with Christopher long enough to know small talk was a rather useless endeavor, but she still liked to try. Every once in a while, she caught a glimmer in his eye that gave her hope that he had the ability to have fun. It would fade almost instantly, but as long as she was working with him, she would continue to pretend that he could smile.

Today, however, he seemed even more on edge than usual. With a *ping*, the elevator reached their floor, and Christopher bolted through the doors before they had even completely opened, Katherine following close behind. He strode down the hallway, oblivious to the employees forced to jump out of the way or those who cowered as he approached. "Why the delay in Glasgow?" he asked as they walked.

"Tanners union dispute," Katherine answered. Christopher wasn't the only one who liked to be prepared.

He nodded. "And Manchester?"

Again, she was ready with the answer. "Waiting for fabric, sir."

If she hadn't known any better, she would have been tempted to believe he wasn't even listening to her answers, that he was just quizzing her. But then Christopher's frown deepened. "And what's Birmingham's excuse?"

Katherine couldn't help herself. He just looked so miserable. "They were attacked by giant fifty-foot spiders," she teased. Lowering her voice, she added, "I blame the Soviets."

That finally got Christopher to look up from the papers in his hand. But instead of offering the light-hearted smile her flippant response deserved, he shook his head. "I don't have time for silliness, Ms. Dane," he replied. His rebuke still hanging in the air, he continued down the hall. He didn't understand why Katherine continued to try and make light when they were at work. Nor did he understand her ability to use something as serious as the Soviet threat as comedic fodder.

They had won the war, but they had come far too close to defeat. He knew. He had been there, on the front lines, facing the enemy head-on. It was hardly a joking matter. He had lost good men, men he had called friends. And he knew he was not alone. The streets of

London, while once again bustling and teeming with energy, were not as full as they had been a few years before. No one had gone untouched by the war. Yet here Katherine was, joking about the next threat to face them. He had once mentioned Katherine's somewhat, well, *casual* approach to authority to his wife, Evelyn, hoping for some sympathy. To his surprise, she had suggested that maybe Katherine was right to not let the war—as devastating as it had been—win. "It took so much from all of us already," she had said. "Why let it take our humor as well?" Christopher had been as baffled by that response as he would have been if Evelyn had spoken it in Ancient Greek.

Shaking his head, Christopher was about to remind Ms. Dane once more that when on the job, there was to be no joking, when Hal Gallsworthy popped out of his office and joined them.

"It's just Birmingham, sir," Hal said, pushing his round glasses farther up the bridge of his nose. "They're always late."

Christopher admired Hal. The man was forthright,

sometimes to a fault. But he could also be oblivious. "I needn't remind you that we're under intense pressure to trim costs," Christopher said as they arrived at the end of the hall. A large set of double doors was closed in front of them. Above the wooden frame was a sign that read: EFFICIENCY DEPARTMENT. Quickly, and one might even say *efficiently*, Christopher pushed open the doors and entered his department.

Once more, Christopher allowed himself the smallest of moments to pause to appreciate the department. Like its name suggested, it was a hub of efficiency. There was not one excess piece of paper, no unneeded clutter, not even a spare desk or chair for a possible visitor. The exact number of needed desks for the employees of the department—twenty in total—lined each side of the large room, ten per side. Behind them sat men, along with several women, wearing spotless suits, their hands busy. There was no room for idleness in this department. Christopher Robin saw to that.

"Mr. Robin!"

Hearing his name, Christopher snapped to immediate

attention. Looking ahead, he saw his senior management team gathered in the middle of the room. In comparison to the neatly ordered lines of desks, their cluster seemed chaotic to Christopher and he couldn't help frowning as he approached.

The team was staring down at what was once a lovely top-of-the-line piece of Wilson luggage. Only now, it looked like something that had been attacked by a very angry bear, or worse. It had been dissected piece by piece until it was nothing but a pile of leather, stitching, torn fabric, and buckles. As Christopher approached, he heard his team discussing the deconstructed luggage. He didn't speak at first, letting their conversation continue. His team had been together for a while and were a cohesive bunch who worked best when they worked together, bouncing ideas back and forth like a Ping-Pong ball.

"If we replace the second inner bevel with beechwood," Matthew Leadbetter was saying in his usual pragmatic way, "we can increase buoyancy by four percent—"

He was interrupted by Joan MacMillan. The only

female member of the group, she could be skittish when pressed but had one of the brightest minds Christopher knew. She was instrumental in keeping the Efficiency Department on track, and when it came to their little group, she was anything but fragile or frightened. "And decrease weight by point-two percent," she said now. The others nodded at her quick calculations.

"And cost?" Christopher said, finally jumping into the conversation, his mind focused on the only thing of true importance. As head of the Efficiency Department, his goal was making sure that they saved the company *lots* of money, if possible.

Ralph Butterworth, the pessimist–or realist, as he liked to call himself–of the group, shrugged his shoulders. "Might save a few shillings," he answered.

That was what Christopher was afraid of. A few shillings were not nearly enough to help the company with its bottom line. But he didn't want to sound too disheartening to the team. "Keep plugging away, everyone," he said, hoping he sounded inspiring when inside he felt rather defeated. "Leave no stone unturned."

To his surprise, his words were met with clapping. "Bravo! That's what I like to hear!"

Turning, the group found themselves looking at their boss, Giles Winslow. At the sudden attention, the young man shifted nervously on his feet and fiddled with the brown accordion folder he held in his hands. While technically the boss, a role he had landed due to being the son of Winslow Sr., he seemed out of his comfort zone here in the Efficiency Department. Unlike his employees, whose pale and worn faces remained glued to the work on their desks, Giles's face was sun-kissed—and there were no signs of bags under his eyes. He was clearly a man who enjoyed the outdoors and didn't spend time worrying about the bottom line of his company. After all, he had employees to do that for him.

"Mr. Winslow, sir," Christopher said, quickly reacting to the slight awkwardness that was now filling the room. "I could have come to your office."

Giles shook his head. "Oh, no, no," he retorted. "I love coming down here, get my hands dirty once in a while . . ." As if to prove his point, he reached out and touched a luggage sample lying on the nearest table.

"That sample is still wet, sir," Christopher said.

As if he had been burned, Giles quickly removed his hand and began to wipe his fingers with a handkerchief he'd pulled from his pocket. Still trying to play the part of someone who had even the faintest of clues, he lifted his head and took a deep sniff of the air. "Ah, the smell of leather!" he said. "The smell of hard work. Much rather be here than in my stuffy office where all the boring stuff happens. Yawn! *This* is where I belong. Down here with the real men—*and* women!" he added hastily. "Yes, I hate offices. Give me some manual labor any day of the week." As he finished, he attempted to lift one foot and put it on a stack of samples that someone had left in a pile. But the moment his foot touched the pile, the samples began to fall with a loud *thud, thud, thud.* "Um, let's go into your office, shall we?" Giles finally said, stepping over the samples and making his way by the senior management team.

Christopher followed, but not before shooting the group a warning look. He knew his team. The second the door to his office closed, they were going to rush over and try to listen in on the conversation.

Sure enough, the door hadn't even clicked shut behind Giles and Christopher before the whole team was crowded in front of it, ears pressed to the wood.

Inside Christopher's office, Giles wasted no time getting to the point. He knew he had just made a fool of himself out there and the sooner he could get out of this horrid department, the better. "We just got the latest sales report," he said, handing Christopher the brown folder he had been carrying and then plopping down into a chair.

With a sense of dread, Christopher opened the folder and began to look through the papers. Numbers in red and black, but mostly red, jumped out at him from the pages, and he felt the blood draining from his face. The room seemed to grow hotter and he found it difficult to breath. Placing two fingers behind the knot of his tie, he struggled to loosen the confining article of clothing. Then he, too, sank into a chair.

Outside the office, the senior management team watched, their eyes wide.

"I'm no body language expert," Leadbetter said, watching his boss closely, "but I'd say—"

"We're all stuffed," Butterworth finished for him.

Gallsworthy, as usual the last to grasp what was going on, tried to push himself closer. "What are they saying?" he asked. "I can't hear."

"Don't worry. I can lip-read," MacMillan answered, putting on a pair of glasses. Then she squinted painfully. "These aren't mine."

As the others groaned, Christopher and Giles continued their "private" conversation. Or rather, Christopher continued worrying and Giles continued to throw judgment his way. "How did things get so bad?" Christopher asked, running a hand through his hair. He just didn't understand. He had been tirelessly efficient. Every *T* had been crossed and every *I* had been dotted—more than once. If there was ever a question about something that *might* not have been efficient, Christopher assumed it wouldn't be and made the appropriate changes to the plan or purchase. Granted, he knew that times were lean for many. The war's effects had reached far beyond the battleground. Luxury purchases were not high on the list of the general population. Still . . .

"You tell me," Giles said, interrupting Christopher's spiraling thoughts. "You're the efficiency expert. Of all my father's businesses, Winslow Luggage is the worst. Embarrassing for me, of course . . ." He looked down at his hand and scrutinized the freshly buffed nails, his behavior the exact opposite of someone feeling at all ashamed. "In short, we need to cut some costs."

Christopher stopped himself from rolling his eyes. Things were bad enough. Getting caught being disrespectful to the boss was the last thing he needed. "It's all I've been working on," he said instead. He gestured out the window of his office toward the department beyond. As he did so, he noticed a group of heads duck down beneath the pane. "And we've made headway. Three percent, or thereabouts."

"We're going to have to cut deeper than three

percent, Robin," Giles said, uncrossing one leg and then crossing the other.

"How much?" Christopher said, dreading the answer before the question had fully come out.

"Twenty."

Whatever blood had been left in his face rushed out; Christopher's heart slammed against his chest. Twenty percent? That was a nearly impossible number. He shook his head. No, it was actually a completely impossible number. His head once again turned to the window. His team had moved away from his office and were standing around Katherine's desk, pretending—poorly—not to be watching. Catching their boss's eyes on them, they all began to fidget with random things on his secretary's desk.

"There must be another way," Christopher said, turning his attention back to his boss. "Your father promised these people there'd be a good job to come home to after the war. They'd do anything for this company. *I'd* do anything for this company." He *wanted* to add that he already pretty much *had* given everything to the company, and he also wanted to ask what exactly it was that *Giles* did to help the company. But he was stopped by Giles getting to his feet.

"My father has called an emergency meeting on Monday," he said, heading toward the door. "We've got to produce the cuts by then."

"I promised my wife and daughter I'd go away this weekend—"

Giles raised an eyebrow. Christopher lowered his head. He *had* just said he would do anything for this company. But he had also promised his wife and their daughter that he would finally take a break and head out to the country house. They hadn't been there in ages, mostly because every time they made plans to visit, Christopher canceled them. And now it looked like he was going to go and ruin yet another weekend. He let out a deep sigh. His wife was patient and understanding, but even she had her limits. And another cancellation? It could very well push her beyond them.

"You have dreams, Robin?" Giles's question surprised him. Christopher looked up, confusion written on his face. "Well, I'll let you in on a little secret. Dreams don't come for free, Robin," he went on, offering advice that Christopher frankly didn't want to hear. "Nothing comes from nothing. And if this ship goes down, you've got to ask yourself, 'Am I a swimmer? Or am I sinker?' "

"Obviously I want to be a swimmer, sir," Christopher replied.

Giles nodded. "Right answer! Me too. That's why I'll be working this weekend also. All hands on deck and all that." Reaching back into the accordion folder, he pulled out a single sheet of paper. He handed it over to Christopher. "A list of names here of people who can 'walk the plank' if you—*we*—don't come up with something. Good luck!"

And with that threat delivered, he opened the door and left Christopher's office.

Christopher stood where Giles had left him, sheet in hand. What was he going to do now?

Chapter Two

Christopher stood in the doorway to his office for a long, painful moment, the paper Giles had handed him seemingly burning in his hand. How was he supposed to go through and just send these people "to the plank" as Giles had so flippantly suggested? These people weren't just numbers to him. They were men and women he worked side by side with, day in and day out. When he had first started, he had done his best to keep them at arm's length. But over time, he had loosened up—slightly. True, he strived to maintain a level of professionalism, but there was no way he could have gone without learning about their families, their struggles, their accomplishments. They were, for all intents and purposes, part of his family. His gaze turned to his senior management team. *Especially* them. While he had still not looked at the names listed on Giles's paper, he had to assume that some of their names would be there. After all, senior management, as the title suggested, had been there the longest and offered the most in terms of skill. They would have the highest salaries. And if Giles was serious about cutting 20 percent? Well, then it didn't take an efficiency expert to know that high-paid employees would be some of the first to go.

Christopher sighed. He couldn't stand in his office doorway denying the inevitable forever, as tempting as the thought might be. And from the anxious looks on the faces of his team, he knew they probably had a very good idea of what had just happened anyway. Bracing himself, Christopher left the office and walked over. "I presume you got most of that?" he said to all of them.

Instantly, he was met with a chorus of hollow denials.

Christopher stifled a smile at the chorus of "Never!" and "No!" flung his way. It was actually rather endearing how unprofessional they had been and how sly they had *thought* they were. He raised an eyebrow knowingly.

"Well, maybe a *little* bit . . ." Butterworth finally

admitted, before filling in Christopher on what they thought they had heard. According to him, the team believed that Giles and Christopher had talked a lot about a "windy tent" and ordering "apples."

If the situation hadn't been so dire, Christopher might have laughed out loud at their horrible interpretation of the actual conversation. Instead, he responded with a wary smile. "Windy tent," he told them, was the 20 percent they would need to cut; and the "apples" he had apparently been ordering was in actuality the *impossible* he had reacted with when Giles told him to reduce staff. Their faces dropped as Christopher continued to fill them in. "Anyone with proposals for cuts, get them to me by tomorrow," he said, wrapping things up. "I'll look over everything this weekend, come up with a plan."

"We'll do our best, sir!" Hastings said for the team, trying, as always, to be positive.

"Thank you," Christopher said genuinely. "I know. But remember, we're the lucky ones. We have jobs. Let's try and keep it that way, shall we?" Then, with one last glance around the room, he walked back into his office, shutting the door behind him. Then he walked over and lowered the shade on his window. He didn't want anyone to risk seeing him as he sat down behind his desk and lowered his head into his hands.

He had just given his team the ultimatum to end all ultimatums. Find a way to make an impossible number happen, or lose your job. He had never in his entire adult life felt like such a horrible person.

Then he remembered that he was going to have to cancel his weekend plans.

Scratch that, he thought, letting out a loud groan. *Now* he truly felt like the most horrible person in the entire world.

* * *

Night had fallen over the city of London. Streetlamps flickered on, casting their dim light over the cobblestones below.

But inside the Winslow Luggage Efficiency Department, every light was on.

Christopher and his team had worked straight through the rest of the day, into the early evening and long after they should have gone home to their own families and dinners. Now they sat hunched over their desks, their heads drooping. Stacks of papers were piled in front of each member of the team. Calculations were written on every surface; some had been scratched out, but others were circled. None of them, however, provided a solution.

Hearing a loud *thunk*, Christopher looked out of his office toward the team that was gathered in the bull pen. Butterworth had fallen asleep, his head falling straight down onto the papers in front of him.

Getting to his feet, Christopher walked over. Placing a hand on Butterworth's shoulder, he gently shook him awake. "Time to go," he said. "Leave your proposals on your desks. I'll collect them later."

A few members of the team attempted to protest, but they were feeble attempts at best; and after another order from Christopher to go, they happily packed up their belongings and headed toward the elevators.

Christopher watched them go before turning, grabbing the proposals they had left behind, and heading back to his office. Their work might have been over for the evening, but Christopher felt—as he looked down at his watch—that he could still get a few more hours in before he went home. At this point, Evelyn and Madeline were most likely asleep anyway.

***

Christopher Robin stayed at the office until the numbers on the pages in front of him began to blur into one another, forming an odd sort of abstract art piece; and still he held out, until he found his own head coming perilously close to slamming onto the top of the desk as he started to fade. Only then did he pack it up for the night. Gathering his own papers, along with the proposals from his team, he put them all in his briefcase and locked it up tight. The last thing he needed after all that work was to have them falling out as he made his way home.

Home. The word sounded equal parts wonderful

and frightening. He wanted nothing more than to walk through the front door, hang up his coat and hat, and then fall into the nearest chair and hopefully get at least a few hours of sleep. At the same time, he dreaded waking up in the morning and having to tell his wife and daughter that he would be missing the weekend in the country—again!

As luck would have it, he was afforded at least a sliver of his homecoming fantasy. Walking through the front door, he *did* manage to hang up his coat and hat. And he *did* make his way in the general direction of the dreamed-of chair. But that was where fantasy and reality split. Because instead of finding a comfy chair and falling immediately asleep, he found two suitcases packed and waiting by the front door—and his wife waiting in the dining room.

Evelyn didn't say anything as she watched her husband enter the room, his eyes tired and his shoulders stooped. He looked, she thought, defeated. As if he were carrying the weight of the world on his slim shoulders. As she had made dinner earlier that evening, she had found herself humming the song that they had danced to at their wedding. Thoughts of the weekend ahead had warmed her cheeks and made her feel almost giddy, like the young woman she had been when she and Christopher first met. Then things had been so easy, so carefree. There had been no war, no pressure from bosses, no mention of "efficiency." They had jumped in the car at the spur of the moment to take off on adventures, and had been content doing even the most mundane of tasks as long as they were together.

But things had grown harder in the past few years. The war had changed her husband and had changed their marriage. When he had returned home, determined to take care of his growing family, Christopher had begun to pull away. Evelyn had tried—she *still* tried—to bring back some of the spontaneity of their old life, some of the joy. But more often than not, work got in the way. She had hoped, as she cooked dinner, that the weekend ahead was going to give them a much-needed break. But then she had gotten the call from the office and knew that the long-delayed break wasn't going to come. Not this weekend, at least. And it made her heart ache—for Christopher, for Madeline, for herself. It would be easier to be disappointed, she thought now as Christopher entered the room, if she didn't still love her husband to the point of distraction.

"Madeline wanted to wait for you," Evelyn said, her voice soft and full of emotion as Christopher caught sight of the lone setting that remained on the table, "but it was getting so late." The rest of the table had been cleared away. The single plate, cup, and silverware set was left behind as a not-so-gentle reminder to Christopher of another thing he had missed. Pulling his gaze from the table, he looked over at his wife, who stood framed in the door between the kitchen and the dining room. Her arms were crossed across her chest, her deep brown eyes made even deeper by unspoken emotion. As he watched, she moved closer, the light from the kitchen catching the lighter highlights in her brown hair and making them glimmer like gold. Christopher couldn't help feeling a rush of love—and the familiar pang and yearning he got whenever he caught sight of Evelyn's beauty. All these years later, every time he saw her, Christopher still felt as if he were seeing her for the first time.

"I'm sorry," Christopher apologized, knowing that it rang false in the hushed dining room. "I was delayed at work."

"I know. Katherine called to let me know," she replied.

Of course, Christopher thought. Her eerie calmness now made a bit more sense. While Evelyn was always the calmer of the two of them, she was also the more passionate *and* the more punctual. Being on time, keeping your word, open communication—all those things were etched deep in Evelyn's rule book. If Katherine, not him, had called Evelyn and told her he was going to be late, he had been in trouble even before he stepped foot through the door at home.

"She *also* said you'd be working this weekend," Evelyn added. Christopher gulped. It was getting worse by the second. "I guess you won't be coming to the cottage." She said it more as a statement of fact than a question.

Christopher sighed. He knew it was useless to try and explain *why* he needed to stay home and work. He knew what she would do. Evelyn would offer to help, or even suggest that he bring some of his work with him. As long as they were together, that was all that mattered, she would say. But Evelyn hadn't seen the look of fear that had crossed over his team members' faces as he told them what would happen if they couldn't make the cuts. He had to focus his undivided attention on the task at hand. He didn't want to let his family down, but he also didn't want to let his team—and the company—down. He was, as the saying went, stuck between a rock and a hard place. "It can't be helped," he finally said.

"It never can," Evelyn replied, giving her husband a sad, rueful smile. She hadn't meant to let her own disappointment leak into her voice, but it had, nonetheless. The look of misery that flashed over his face made her regret the words instantly. Christopher might pretend to be tough and hardened, but Evelyn knew that deep down, he cared—immensely. Unfortunately, she couldn't take back her words, and while they may have hurt, there was truth in them. Sighing, Evelyn walked from the doorway back into the kitchen. "Why don't you go and break the news to your daughter while I reheat your dinner?"

Christopher watched her go. For a long moment, he didn't move. Facing his upset wife was no walk in the park. But disappointing his daughter? That was going to be awful. A part of him had hoped that by getting home this late, he would have been able to avoid seeing her that night. Letting out a deep sigh, he headed toward the stairs.

The Robins' London home was no longer the opulent and polished place it had been when Christopher was a boy. The years after his father's death—which had happened shortly after he started at boarding school—had been hard on his mother and on their finances. It was, in many ways, why Christopher felt obligated to give Winslow Luggage so much of his time. They had offered him a job when he was young and inexperienced, giving him a way to keep the family afloat.

When he and Evelyn had married, they had moved into the Robins' city home. But things remained tight, so the more superficial needs—touching up chipping paint or refreshing crumpling wallpaper—often were not attended to. Still, Evelyn had managed to make the house warm and inviting, and it had been, for a time, the hub for many a fun and lively dinner party. Then the war had happened and everything had changed.

Walking up the steep front staircase, Christopher smiled sadly as he passed the photo of his parents that hung on the wall. In it, they were both smiling at something off camera. They were clearly happy, their relaxed postures so different from the stiff, serious ones Christopher remembered from his youth. He wondered now, not for the first time, if that was how Madeline would look at pictures of her parents. Would she wonder what had happened to make them so serious?

As he reached his daughter's door, Christopher had a brief flickering hope that she might have already fallen asleep, saving him from the conversation he was dreading. But the light that seeped out from under the door and the faint mumbling he heard coming from the other side dashed that hope as quickly as it had been ignited. Knocking, he entered Madeline's room.

The young girl was sitting on her bed. It was clear she had started to go to sleep, though something had kept her up. And seeing the large box in front of her, its contents spilled all over the duvet and the excited look in her eyes, he had a pretty good sense of what exactly that something was.

"What do you have there?" Christopher asked.

Madeline looked up, startled by her father's sudden appearance in her doorway. She blushed guiltily, her angelic cheeks turning red and looking even sweeter. "Oh, it's yours," she answered shyly. "I found it in the attic. It has loads of stuff from when you were young."

As he took a step closer, Christopher's eyes widened. The box, which he had mistaken for an ordinary box, was indeed his, from when he was a boy. Specifically, it was the box he had packed up the morning he left their country home and had completely forgotten about. Looking at the objects Madeline had strewn over the bed, he saw smooth river pebbles, a few sticks, and several drawings, the childish sketches having grown faint over the years. Madeline reached down and pulled out a small bag. Her movement caused it to open, and out spilled a handful of small brown acorns.

"Haycorns," Christopher said before he could stop himself. Shaking his head, he quickly corrected his mistake. "I mean, acorns. Nothing important. Shouldn't you be doing something more useful with your time?" He asked. He suddenly didn't like the curious way Madeline was looking at him. He needed a distraction. Looking around the room, he noticed the pile of textbooks next to her bed. "Like reading, perhaps?" He pointed to the books.

Madeline was quick with a response. Like her father, she prided herself on keeping on task. "I'm already finished with the booklist Grayford Prep sent." At her father's pleased nod, she added, "I'm way ahead. I've been very efficient."

"Good," Christopher replied. "That's good." Sending his daughter to the same boarding school he had attended as a boy was a luxury they really couldn't afford, but Madeline was a *Robin*. And the Robins had been going to Grayford for generations. It was yet another reason why he was going to be stuck at the office all weekend. He couldn't afford to lose his job. Not now, especially.

"Yes," Madeline said, happy to have pleased her father. "But there's no work to do this weekend. We can do whatever we want. Puzzles, board games?" Her voice rose hopefully.

Christopher could barely stand to meet his daughter's gaze. Her blue eyes were wide and innocent, the look he saw in them a painful reminder of the toll his job, his life, was taking on his family. He had seen that look, years ago now, reflected in the mirror when he had been a child. Talking to his own father about the adventures he had had in the woods behind their country house, begging him to come along and always being met with a firm no. He wondered, not for the first time, how he had become that very same man. But what choice did he have? If he wanted to provide any kind of future for his child, he had to work. Looking down, he absently played with an acorn, eager for any reason to break eye contact with his daughter. "About that . . ." he finally said. "I can't go this weekend."

"But summer will be over soon," Madeline said, her voice beginning to quiver. "I never see you."

"I know," he said, the words catching in his throat. Just then, an image of Giles, accordion folder in hand, flashed through his mind—and he sat up straighter. "I wish I didn't have to work, but you know, dreams don't come for free, Madeline. You have to work for them. Nothing comes from nothing. You understand?" Even as the words came out of his mouth, Christopher hated himself for using them. It was one thing for Giles to lecture him about working. There was no reason he should be saying these things to his young daughter.

To his shame and horror, the hope faded from Madeline's eyes and she nodded slowly. "I understand," she said softly. Then, picking up the acorns, she handed them to him. "I suppose you can keep these here then. Do you think you could read to me for a minute?"

"Oh," Christopher said, startled by the request. That was usually something Evelyn did with Madeline before bedtime. "Well, yes. Of course," he added. Reaching over, he pulled one of her school books from the pile and opened it to the first page. He had already started reading and therefore did not notice that Madeline had chosen her own book—a fairy tale.

"Actually, Father," she said after listening to the dry historical narrative for a few moments, "I'm a bit tired." As if to prove her point, she let out a very loud, very fake yawn and started to snuggle down under the covers.

Christopher narrowed his eyes at the yawn and opened his mouth to say something, but decided against it. Getting to his feet, he awkwardly tapped his daughter on the shoulder and then turned to leave. "Good night, then," he said, flicking off the light and throwing the room into darkness.

Behind him, Madeline said a quiet good night and turned over so her back was to him. With one last look at his daughter, Christopher sighed and shut the door.

Sweet dreams, he added silently. The apology he wanted to offer stayed stuck in his throat. It was probably for the best. If he wanted his daughter to rest well, she didn't need to hear any more hollow excuses. . . .

* * *

"I was thinking," Christopher said. "You two don't *have* to go tomorrow."

He was sitting at the dining room table, eating the supper that Evelyn had reheated for him. The house was quiet, the only sounds coming from the clinking of his silverware against the china and the creaking floor boards as the old building settled on its foundation. Evelyn sat at the other end of the table from her husband, not speaking. Christopher had tried to ignore the dark looks being sent his way until the silence had grown uncomfortable and he had finally spoken.

"We've been over this," Evelyn said, obviously unimpressed by her husband's suggestion. "She needs to play, Christopher, not spend all her time studying."

"Grayford Prep is the best," Christopher replied, not

looking up from his plate. "She's doing the reading."

Evelyn took a deep breath. She loved her husband. And *had* loved him practically from the first moment she met him. She loved that he was a hard worker, and dedicated and trustworthy. She loved that he cared about the future, and she loved that he wanted the best for his daughter. But what she didn't love, what she couldn't understand, was how he could also be so uptight and narrow-minded. The man she had met and fallen in love with all those years ago had had at least a spark of imagination. He had smiled and laughed and been willing to have fun and be spontaneous. But the man sitting across from her now? Sometimes she didn't even recognize him. Her feelings aside, though, what mattered now was their daughter.

"She'd do anything to please you," Evelyn said, trying to keep her voice level. The last thing she wanted to do was let her emotions get in the way. "But there are perfectly good schools in London that don't require us to send her away. And you know she doesn't want to go."

Christopher looked up. "I went away at her age," he

replied matter-of-factly. "It'll prepare her for the real world. Set her up for a career. Isn't that our responsibility to her?" Evelyn shot him a look.

"What?" he asked.

Getting to her feet, Evelyn pushed back her chair and walked over to her husband. She sat down in front of him and took his hands in hers. "You don't even like your job," she said softly, looking into his eyes.

"What has that got to do with anything?"

"*I* didn't go to Grayford and I actually like what I do," Evelyn pointed out.

"Yes, but what you do is more of a hobby, isn't it?" Christopher asked.

Evelyn raised a perfectly arched eyebrow. A spark of fire flared in her eyes and her cheeks flushed. She loved her husband. With all her heart. But there were times—like now—when he said things that made her want to scream in frustration. Her *hobby*, as Christopher called her job, was so much more than that. It was something that helped pay the bills, but more importantly, it was something that actually inspired her. She loved going to work. She loved working with the team of engineers and architects and builders hired by the city. When she was at the office, people respected her opinion, they laughed at her jokes, they engaged in conversation. She was valued. At home, she was lucky these days if she and Christopher even had the chance to speak more than a few sentences to each other. She let out a deep sigh and curbed her full response. This was not the time to bicker. "Half the city was destroyed during the Blitz," she said instead, trying to keep her tone neutral. "I'm trying to help rebuild it. That's what the government grant is for."

"You've got a grant from the government?" Christopher asked, sounding surprised.

"I told you this *weeks* ago," Evelyn answered. She let go of her husband's hands and put her own down in her lap. When she spoke again, she didn't bother to try to hide the sadness. "This is what I'm talking about. Even when you're here, you're not here. You're going to hit your limit. One day, you're going to crack."

"If I work hard now, then in the future life will be—" He lifted his fork to take a bite.

Evelyn didn't give him the chance. She had heard enough excuses for one evening and her patience had run out. Yanking his food away, she glared at him. "Will be what?" she asked. "Better? Worse? We don't care. We'd rather have *you. This* is life, Christopher. Life is happening right now. In front of you. Look, yoo-hoo!" She raised her arms in the air and waved them around, all the while making a goofy face. Christopher didn't even crack a smile. Evelyn lowered her arms and sighed. "I haven't seen you laugh in years."

"I found that very amusing," Christopher replied flatly.

Evelyn stood up. Picking up his plate, she began to move toward the kitchen but stopped before she got to the door. Turning, she looked back at her husband. He was still sitting, a look of confusion on his face. "I just want to see you have fun sometimes. Be a little silly. I didn't fall for you because you were 'set up for a career.' "

Getting up from his seat, Christopher sighed. "Please don't make this harder on me," he said softly. "I am sorry." He turned and looked toward the front hall, where the suitcases stood, waiting to be put in the car in the morning. "I'll take my suitcase back upstairs. I'm sorry I asked you to pack mine." But when he walked over, he realized it wasn't even there. "Where is mine?"

"I didn't even bother," Evelyn said. And with that, she turned and walked into the kitchen, the door swinging shut behind her. In the front hall, Christopher remained, staring down at the suitcases. His wife's purposeful lack of action on this matter spoke louder than any of the words she had said at the dinner table and hit harder than any punch she could have thrown. What had happened to them? How had it come to this? There was a time when they would have been able to find a way to laugh at the situation. There was a time when Evelyn would have been his source of comfort, when he would have spoken up, shared his fears of what would happen to his team. But now? Now there was no intimacy to their words, no passion behind their conversations. Christopher knew he was to blame for most of it. Evelyn was patient and kind and wonderful, and he knew she loved him. But he had kept her at an arm's length for so long now that he didn't quite know how to shorten the distance. *What if,* he thought as he finally turned and headed upstairs to bed, *I can't get her back? What if she's right? What if I can't have fun anymore?*

* * *

Christopher slept poorly that night. He tossed and turned, odd images flashing through his mind, tugging at his memory and making him shout out in his sleep. Woods, eerie and ghostly, filled the dreams—and through the thick fog that surrounded the trees and covered the floor, he could just make out the barest outlines of bears and rabbits, donkeys and pigs.

He woke with a start, sweat covering his brow, and turned to where his wife's warm body usually lay. But the far side of the mattress was cold. Opening his eyes, he saw weak sunlight filtering through the curtains. Day had broken. From downstairs, he heard the sound of the front door opening and his daughter's voice mingling with that of Evelyn's. They were getting ready to leave.

Pushing back the covers, Christopher hastily threw on work clothes and headed downstairs. As he had guessed, the front door was open. Through it he could see the car waiting, the boot already packed with Madeline's and Evelyn's bags. The pair were in the living room and barely afforded him a look when he joined them.

"Well," he said awkwardly. "Have a nice time." Reaching down, he tried to give Madeline a hug but her body was stiff in his arms, so he just gave her a quick peck on the cheek and a few pats on the back.

In return, the little girl gave a weak nod and started to walk away. But she paused. Turning back to him, she handed him a folded-up piece of paper. "I love this drawing of yours," she said, her voice soft. "Maybe you could put it next to mine?" At his nod, she smiled weakly and then headed outside.

Evelyn waited for her to be out the door before saying her own cold, quick good-bye to Christopher. He wasn't sure if it was intentional or not, but the quick peck on the cheek and brief pat on the back that showed no warmth or emotion felt like an unspoken punishment for how he had handled his own good-bye—how he had handled everything. Without another word, Evelyn followed her daughter out the door. Christopher went and watched as they both got in and drove away.

"I'm sorry," he mumbled, raising a hand in farewell. But he knew it was too late. No apology would make up for him missing this weekend. With a sigh, he turned and headed back into the house. Entering the kitchen, he lifted his briefcase and placed it on the counter. The teakettle began to squeal and he absently made himself a cup. Then, with his trademark efficiency, he opened the briefcase and scanned the contents to make sure he had everything he would need for the task at hand. Pulling the paper Madeline had given him from his pocket, he unfolded it. To his surprise, looking back at him from the page was a drawing of his old friend Winnie the Pooh.

A jolt shot through him and his odd dreams from the night before came back. Goose bumps covered his arms as he stared down at the bear. He hadn't thought of him in years. Yet seeing the image now, he felt like he could almost hear the bear, smell the Hundred-Acre Wood. A slow smile began to spread over his face. . . .

And then, out in the front hall, the grandfather clock chimed loudly. Christopher startled, his smile disappearing. He put the drawing down and, grabbing his briefcase, hurriedly headed toward the front door, bumping the table as he went. A small jar of honey, left out and open from Madeline's breakfast, fell over on its side. Unaware of the spill, Christopher exited the house, slamming the door as he went.

In the kitchen, the honey jar began to roll, sent into motion by the vibration of the slamming door. Honey spilled out, oozing over the wooden table and then onto the drawing of Pooh. A moment later, it crashed to the floor, the sound of pottery oddly loud in the now quiet house. . . .

Chapter Three

Pooh awoke with a mumble, a grumble, and then a small sniffle. Slowly, he opened his eyes. His red sleep cap was askew on his head, and as he fully awakened, he stretched a long, hard stretch. He felt as though he had been asleep for years. He shivered, feeling oddly cold until slowly warmth began to spread through him. Sitting up, he sniffed the air. Something smelled very, very good.

"*Mmmmm,*" he said. "Honey."

The smell lured him out of bed and he walked across his room toward the dresser that stood in the far corner. His image peered back at him from the full-length mirror beside the dresser. He cocked his head, taking in his rumpled fur and disheveled nightcap. Smoothing down his fur, he frowned. Something didn't feel right. He was confused. More confused, rather, than usual.

"I've forgotten what to do," he said, looking around the room. Then his eyes brightened as he took in the kitchen cupboards. "Ah, yes!" he exclaimed happily. "Time to make myself hungry with my stoutness exercise." Bending over, he began to stretch his front paws down toward his feet. Then he raised himself up and did it again. As he continued his stoutness exercises, he sang a little song:

Up down, up.
When I up, down, touch the ground,
It puts me in the mood.
When I up, down, touch the ground,
In the mood for food.

On cue, his tummy let out a loud rumble. His morning exercise routine done, he eagerly made his way over to the cupboard. Reaching up, he opened it and cringed at the loud squeak that followed. If he hadn't known any better, he would have said he hadn't opened that particular cupboard in a very long time. But that would be impossible. This was the honey cupboard, and he had honey every day. Pulling the door open the rest of the way, he smiled at the large row of pots that greeted him. Each one read HUNNY on the side. His belly rumbled in anticipation as he grabbed one. But to his horror, when he reached inside, he found that the jar was empty. He grabbed another one and opened it. It was empty, too. Tossing it over his shoulder, he grabbed another, and another, and still another.

They were *all* empty.

"Bother," Pooh said. "Somebody seems to have eaten all the honey." Then he raised a paw. "But! There's always an emergency smackerel hiding Somewhere." Sure enough, at the very back of the cupboard, hidden behind still more empty honey pots, was a jar labeled AM URGANCEE HUNNY. Closing his eyes and smacking his lips in eager anticipation of the sweet sugary goodness that was about to make his mouth and tummy very happy, Pooh stuck his paw into the jar. But when he pulled it out, he saw that his paw was not covered in golden goodness. It was not covered in anything. Lifting the jar to his face, Pooh looked inside, squinting his eyes, trying to see if there was even the smallest dollop of honey that perhaps his paw just hadn't reached. He stuck his head still farther in, until with a *pop!* his whole head went into the jar.

For several moments, Pooh stood there, pot stuck, trying to dislodge his head. Finally, with another *pop!* it came free. Stuck to the end of his nose was a note that read: POOH, IOU AM URGANCEE HUNNY POT. SIGNED, POOH.

Pooh frowned. His tummy rumbled, louder this time. This was not good. Not good at all. He had done his exercises, and as such was now very, very hungry. He put a paw to his Thinking Spot and began to tap. *Honey, honey, honey.* Where could he get more honey? Then he had an idea! "Perhaps Piglet's am urgancee hunny hasn't yet been eaten by either me or this other Pooh who thought ahead and wrote that note." He would just have to take himself down to Piglet's and ask his friend.

Quickly putting on his red shirt, Pooh opened the front door. But he stopped before stepping outside. If it weren't for his need for honey, he probably would have liked to have stayed inside. It was a gloomy and grey day. Fog hovered over the ground, making it hard to see. And it was quiet. At least, it was until Pooh's tummy rumbled again. Hesitating, Pooh weighed his options: stay inside and avoid the icky day but be hungry, or take his chances and get to Piglet's and find honey.

He didn't hesitate long. Pooh stepped out into the fog.

It didn't take the bear long to reach his friend's home in the base of a large beech-tree. But while the brown door looked the same and the small window above it was open, there was something very empty-looking about Piglet's house. The sign that stood to the side of the front door, with the words TRESPASSWERS W, hung askew, and the carved words were hard to read through the moss that had begun to grow in them. Pooh hesitated. The whole place felt . . . forgotten.

Pooh walked up and knocked on the door. "Piglet?" he called out. "It's Pooh. Are you home?" There was no answer.

Pushing open the door, Pooh peered inside. Sure enough, Piglet was not home. He frowned. Where would his friend be on such a grey day? Once again, he put his paw to his Thinking Spot. "Think, think, think," he said. "Who would want to be alone on a day like today?" He stopped tapping his head. That was it! No one would want to be alone! Piglet must have gone to find one of their other friends. Shutting Piglet's door, he turned and headed back into the woods. He would try Eeyore's next.

Not surprisingly, Eeyore's Gloomy Place—as he liked to call his home—was, as usual, rather gloomy. And in the fog, it was even gloomier. It was also quiet, just like it had been back at Pooh's, and as the bear wandered through the boggy area, he saw that it, too, seemed run-down. Just like Piglet's house. "Eeyore?" Pooh called out. There was no answer. Neither of his friends were there.

Maybe, he thought, leaving the gloomy bog, they had gone to find Rabbit. Rabbit always had the answers for everything. Maybe they had gone to ask him why the Hundred-Acre Wood seemed so . . . well, abandoned.

But when he arrived at Rabbit's house, it was empty, too. "Rabbit!" he shouted. "I require an answer!" Usually that got Rabbit right out of his hole. The stuffy old animal rather enjoyed being the one to tell people things. Only this time, Rabbit's head didn't appear, and when Pooh dared to stick his own head down the hole—the very same one that he had ended up trapped in on more than one fateful occasion—he found Rabbit's den as empty as Piglet's and Eeyore's living areas had been. "Oh, bother," Pooh muttered. "Where is everybody?"

And so it continued as Pooh wandered through the vast Hundred-Acre Wood. No matter where he went, he couldn't find a single soul. "*Hellooo?*" he called out as he walked along. "Can anyone hear me? Kanga or Roo? Tigger? Owl?" No one answered. The only voice he heard was his own, echoing back to him from all around. Wrapping his arms around himself, he shivered. Then he tugged his red shirt down over his belly. What had happened to his friends?

Pooh didn't know what to do. Whenever there was

a problem, his friends would help him solve it. But now there was a problem and no friends. What was he to do? If only Christopher Robin were still around. He would have been able to help. But come to think of it, where had Christopher Robin gone? Pooh hadn't seen him in an awfully long time. . . .

Suddenly, through the fog, Pooh made out a flash of color. A gust of wind blew and the color became clearer. Green. He was looking at a green door in the base of a large old tree. Another gust of wind hit the tree and the door cracked open with a loud *creak*. Pooh smiled. He knew that door! "The Door Through Which Christopher Robin Is Known to Appear!" he cried, inching forward. The green paint was chipping and the door itself was covered with vines; a pile of leaves lined the bottom. "Christopher Robin, are you there?" Pooh called out.

As if in answer, the wind kicked up another notch. The door swung completely open.

Forgetting to be scared, Pooh hurried forward and peered into the darkness. "Christopher Robin?" he called again. "It's me, Winnie the Pooh. Are you finally home?" There was no answer. Pulling back, Pooh tapped his Thinking Spot once again. "Think, think, think," he muttered. What to do, what to do? He thought about his missing friends. Then he thought about the door that had suddenly appeared. He thought about honey—but only for a second. And then he realized he knew what had to be done. He had to find Christopher Robin! "Ah, yes," he said triumphantly. "Christopher Robin will help me find everybody, or help everybody find me. That will be the Order of Looking for Things."

Pushing aside the vines and dead leaves, Pooh took a deep breath. And then, before he could scare himself out of it, he headed through the door into the darkness beyond.

* * *

A moment later, Pooh's head popped out from the hollow part of an old tree trunk. The bear looked around. He was still outside. But he was not in the Hundred-Acre Wood anymore. For one thing, the fog was gone and the sun was shining. For another, he could hear birds chirping in the sky above. And for yet another thing, from what he could tell by looking around, he was in a garden, not in the middle of the woods.

"Christopher Robin?" Pooh called out. "Hello?"

There was no answer. Pulling the rest of his body free from the tree trunk, Pooh began to wander. If the green door was the Door Through Which Christopher Robin Is Known to Appear, it seemed only reasonable that Christopher Robin *should* be somewhere on the other side of the door. Therefore, Pooh had to look for him.

He wandered all around the garden, peeking behind bushes and bird fountains. No Christopher Robin! He wandered by a very large house with lots of doors and quite a few windows. But still no Christopher Robin. Seeing a green gate, he walked up to it and pushed it open. On the other side of the gate was a long drive that lined the garden. "If I were Christopher Robin," the bear asked himself as he made his way down the drive, "where would I be?"

Upon reaching the end of the drive, Pooh stood for a moment. He didn't quite know what to do. He knew that Christopher Robin had to be somewhere, because he had come through the door *Christopher* came through. But Pooh had never been beyond the Hundred-Acre Wood, and he was feeling rather nervous. And hungry. It was hard to think clearly with his tummy rumbling.

Just then, two young girls passed in front of him. They looked around the same age as Christopher. Maybe *they* were going toward his friend. He began to follow them. As he walked, noisy contraptions on wheels began to appear, making loud honking noises as they moved past. He lost sight of the two girls, instead finding himself wandering among the legs of very tall boys and girls. "These woods are very busy," he said, stopping as people rushed around him. "Who is chasing all these people?" Yet, while Pooh was noticing everyone and everything, no one appeared to be noticing him. That is, until, he came face-to-face with a large dog. The creature raised its lips and snarled.

"I'm looking for Christopher Robin," Pooh said,

unaware that the dog was not pleased by his appearance. "Have you seen him?" In response, the dog snarled louder. Then Pooh noticed a large carrot on a cart just out of the dog's reach. "Oh!" he said, understanding the dog's behavior immediately. "You're hungry, too?" Reaching up, he grabbed the carrot and gave it to the dog. The dog wagged his tail and began to munch on the carrot. Pooh smiled. "I must introduce you to my friend Rabbit. If I can find him."

Saying a quick good-bye to the now happy dog, Pooh continued down the street. He so desperately wanted to find his friend. But no matter where he looked, there was no Christopher Robin. He peered behind a large red fire hydrant. He glanced through open doors–none of which were green. He checked under a table with three black hats sitting on top, but all he found was a bunch of fake flowers and a bunch of holes in the top of the table. When he popped his head through one, he found himself staring at a crowd of kids who were watching a strange-looking man in a cape make odd gestures with his hands. Seeing Pooh, the kids let out squeals of delight. "Oh, bother," he said, ducking his head back down and stumbling out from under the table.

Just as Pooh was beginning to lose hope that anything good would come of this adventure, a bee flew over his head. On cue, Pooh's tummy let out a loud rumble. "Hello, bee," he said in delight. "Oh, please tell me you have a honey tree." Craning his head back so he wouldn't lose sight of the buzzing insect, he began to follow it. It made a zigzagging route through the streets. Pooh tried to keep up, but several times he almost lost the bee as he had to duck and weave around the people cluttering the sidewalk. Finally, the bee flew up and over a fence, disappearing from sight into the very same garden that Pooh had departed from not long ago. "Oh," he said, somewhat deflated.

His tummy rumbled. And rumbled again, louder. He knew he should keep looking for Christopher Robin, but he was growing so weak. He couldn't go on. Not unless he found some honey. Or took a nap. Pushing open the gate, he once again entered the garden and then meandered over to the shadiest tree he could find. Plopping down, he leaned back against it. Yes, that was it. He would just rest his eyes for a moment. Then, once he was rested, he could continue looking for Christopher . . . and honey.

* * *

Christopher stood up and stretched. His back let out an angry crack. He had been hunched over his desk since he had arrived at Winslow Luggage earlier that morning, not even taking a break for lunch or to use the bathroom. Unfortunately, all the hard work had resulted in little progress. He was no closer to cutting costs. And, from the looks of his exhausted and defeated team hunched over their desks, they had had no better luck. Walking by, he ordered them all to go home and then decided to leave himself. All he wanted to do was go home, pour himself a drink, and crawl into bed.

But to his dismay, as he got off the double-decker bus in front of his home, he caught sight of his neighbor, Cecil, loitering in front of his house. The man had been after Christopher for months now to finish a game of chess that he had unwittingly entered into at a house party. He had made the mistake of leaving the game unfinished, and Cecil apparently did not like things left unfinished. The very last thing Christopher needed after the day that he'd had was a run-in with Cecil. Quickly, he ducked through the green gate that led into the garden.

Lost in thought, Christopher made his way across the garden and sat, with a thunk, on a bench underneath the largest tree in the garden. He dropped his head into his hands. On the other side of the tree, Winnie the Pooh awoke from his nap. Realizing he was still hungry and thinking he was still no closer to finding his friend, he, too, put his head in his paws.

"Oh, what to do?" Christopher said, sighing.

"What to do indeed," Pooh said, answering the question he hadn't even been asked.

Christopher's head snapped up. That voice! He knew that voice. Turning around, Christopher's eyes widened. "Pooh?!"

"Christopher Robin!" Pooh shouted back. His shout was much happier-sounding than Christopher's.

Jumping to his feet, Christopher began to back away. "No, no, you can't be here," he said, holding up his hands. "You can't be here! This can't be happening." He began to pace up and down. There had to be a rational and reasonable explanation for why his childhood friend, a talking bear, had suddenly appeared in this garden. Maybe the sandwich he had eaten earlier while bent over papers had been bad? He hadn't even looked to see what he was eating. Although if that were the culprit, wouldn't it be his stomach that was acting up, not his head? He kept thinking: Perhaps there was something in the air? Could he be dreaming? He pinched himself. Nope. That wasn't it. Then it came to him. "It's the stress," he said out loud. "I'm exhausted. Oh, God. Evelyn warned me." As he spoke, he began to circle the bench.

That wasn't the best idea. He ended up coming face-to-face with Pooh. The bear smiled up at him happily. "I've cracked," Christopher said. "I've totally cracked."

"I don't see any cracks," Pooh said. He reached up a paw and ever so gently touched Christopher's hand. "A few wrinkles, maybe."

The observation was so simple and so classically Pooh that Christopher felt the sudden need to sit as it began to occur to him that this was really happening. His childhood friend *was* here. In front of him. The feel of the bear's warm paw only served to solidify the thought. The moment his paw touched Christopher's hand, it felt like he was right back in the Hundred-Acre Wood. "Pooh?" he finally said, finding his voice. It shook with wonder, and a fair amount of shock. "You're here? How are you here, Pooh?"

"Well, I went through the Door Through Which Christopher Robin Is Known to Appear. And now, I am here." He said it with absolute innocence, as if it were the most obvious explanation.

Christopher found himself nodding until he remembered something. "But the tree I remember was in the woods behind the country cottage. Not here in London."

"I suppose it's where it needs to be," Pooh replied with a shrug.

Not quite ready to believe all of this, Christopher began to circle the large tree. He looked at the base. He looked up near the branches. He looked on all sides. "But there's no opening," he finally said. "No door on the other side."

"Oh?" Pooh said, shrugging. "We must not need it anymore."

"That's a silly explanation," Christopher replied.

Pooh smiled proudly. "Why, thank you." Then he frowned, taking in the serious expression on his friend's face and the way he crossed his arms sternly as he turned and continued to stare at the tree. "Are you glad to see me, Christopher Robin?" he asked softly.

The question startled Christopher. It was such a serious question from his usually unserious friend. Turning, he gazed down at the bear. Pooh's big eyes looked up at him. A warmth began to spread through Christopher as memories of a long-ago time unearthed themselves in his mind. He *was* happy to see his old friend, he realized. Or at least as happy as he got these days. He opened his mouth to tell him so, but suddenly, he heard the sound of footsteps. A moment later, Cecil Hungerford rounded the corner.

"Well, hello there!" the nosy neighbor called out.

Just in the nick of time, Christopher managed to shove Pooh under his oversized coat. Then he put his hat over the bear's head. Unfortunately, Pooh didn't take too kindly to his new location and struggled in Christopher's arms, making the overcoat shimmy.

"What have you got there, secret Susan?" Cecil said, coming closer and trying to get a look under Christopher's overcoat.

Christopher turned his body so that Pooh was farther from the neighbor's prying eyes. "Just a cat," he said, coming up with a story on the fly. "Definitely a cat. We just got it."

"Ooh," Cecil said, looking, to Christopher's horror, even more interested. "Can I stroke it? I love cats."

"Not this one," Christopher said hastily. The man was incorrigible. Why wouldn't he just take the hint and leave? "This is a nasty, diseased cat. A biter." That finally seemed to get through to Cecil and he took several steps back. Christopher did the same so that the two men were now standing awkwardly several feet from each other. Christopher nodded over his shoulder toward the house. "I was just taking it inside for some milk. Rehabilitate it."

Inside his coat, Pooh, who had stopped moving briefly, distracted by a zipper, resumed his thrashing. "You're squishing me!" he shouted. The protest came out as a mumble, but it was still loud enough for Cecil to hear.

"What the–?" Cecil said, giving Christopher a confused look.

Christopher tried not to groan. This little meeting needed to come to an end. Fast. "I said that," he quickly explained. "Sometimes my voice sounds like that." He cleared his throat and spoke his next words as Pooh-like as possible. "You're squishing me . . . with your demands to play chess."

The explanation was lame but apparently seemed to placate Cecil, who, with one last look at Christopher (and his coat), finally turned to go. "Tomorrow then," he said over his shoulder. "After all, we've got all weekend."

Christopher nodded—already coming up with excuses to get out of the game he had just locked himself into—and then hurried through the garden and into the house.

CHAPTER FOUR

"This is very good," Winnie the Pooh said through a mouthful of honey. "Are you sure that you wouldn't like some, Christopher Robin?"

Christopher looked around the kitchen counter. It was covered in empty honey jars: small jars, large jars, decorative jars, and plain jars. It hadn't mattered what form the honey came in; as soon as Winnie the Pooh found honey, it was eaten. But while the bear seemed to be completely un-bothered by his presence in London, or the very close encounter with Cecil that they had only narrowly escaped, Christopher was the opposite. He was, put simply, freaking out.

He had spent the past thirty minutes, while Pooh ate, trying to wrap his head around everything. He didn't know what was going on or why it was happening. But Pooh was most certainly real and most certainly there. And while the bear looked *slightly* worse for wear, with his fur a bit threadbare and the pads of his paws a bit shabby, he was still most undoubtedly the bear from Christopher's childhood. "Pooh," he asked, the question that had really been perplexing him popping out, "how did you recognize me? After all these years?"

"Oh, you haven't changed at all," Pooh said, not looking up from the honey jar.

"I've changed *tremendously*!" Christopher exclaimed. It was true. He had been a boy when he'd left the Hundred-Acre Wood. A young, innocent boy who'd believed in the impossible and hadn't spent his days worrying about cutting costs and finding the most efficient way to manage a team.

The bear shook his head. "Not right here," he said, reaching up and motioning toward Christopher's eyes. As he did so, honey smeared across the man's cheeks and dripped down onto the ground. "It's still you looking out," he added.

Christopher sighed. Wouldn't it be nice if that were true? But despite what the lovable and kindhearted bear said, he *had* changed. And as he winced at the puddles of honey on the floor and the mess that Pooh made as he jumped off his stool directly *into* the honey, he knew the changes weren't for the better. The Christopher Robin Pooh had known in the Hundred-Acre Wood would have jumped right in the honey puddle with his friend. Instead, the mess made him cringe and he found himself rushing over to the sink to wipe his own sticky face clean before following the bear.

Unaware that his paws were trailing honey, Pooh—who was finally feeling full and therefore more energized—began to explore the London town house. He wandered out of the kitchen and into the dining room before entering the library. He raised a paw and ran it along the book spines as he walked. "This place is very big," he observed. "Do you live here all alone?"

Christopher frantically wiped at the books. "No," he said, shaking his head. Then he paused. "Well, right now, yes. But usually no. My wife and daughter are in the country for the weekend." It felt funny, he realized, to tell the bear that he had a wife and child.

"Why aren't you with them?" Pooh asked. The revelation that his friend was now a parent and husband did not seem to faze the bear. As he waited for an answer, Pooh walked into the drawing room and right onto the fancy rug Evelyn had spent a tidy sum on. The rug began to drag behind him, stuck to the bottom of Pooh's foot.

"I had to stay for work," Christopher answered. "'Why aren't *you* in the country?' is more the question." As he spoke, he reached down and yanked the rug free of Pooh's foot, sending the bear tumbling forward. Pooh landed headfirst in the brass horn part of the family's gramophone. A record began to play.

"Because," Pooh said, his voice now muffled by the musical contraption, "there's nobody Anywhere, and I looked Everywhere."

Christopher lifted the gramophone off the bear's face. Pooh looked back at him, un-bothered by his run-in with the instrument but clearly upset about his missing friends.

"I'm afraid I don't know where they've gone," Christopher said softly. "And even if I did, what can I do? I'm sorry, Pooh." He let out an involuntary yawn, his eyes moving toward the clock on the desk. "It's getting late, and I'm tired, so—" The sound of snoring filled the room, and he turned.

Pooh was fast asleep on a chair.

Walking over, Christopher looked down at his childhood friend. He looked so peaceful and sweet, without a care in the world. *I wonder when the last time I slept like that was?* Christopher thought as he gently lifted Pooh in his arms and made his way upstairs to Madeline's room. With one hand, he drew back the duvet and then lowered the bear into bed. Pooh mumbled in his sleep before turning on his side and resuming his soft snoring.

For a moment, Christopher just stood there. He couldn't remember the last time he had just watched his own daughter sleep. He was always so tired himself when he got home. Or busy. It never occurred to him to take the time to enjoy the innocent peace of a sleeping child. And while Pooh was technically not a child, he was most certainly innocent. As he watched now, Christopher was flooded with thoughts of his own childhood—of the wonderful feeling of falling into bed after a full day of playing in the woods with Pooh and the others. Of snuggling down under the covers to listen to his mother read him a story . . . His eyes drifted over toward Madeline's bookcase, and as they did, they landed on the box that Madeline had found in the attic.

Tiptoeing over, Christopher opened the box and peered inside. There were a few acorns, a twig, and a small piece of cloth he *thought* might have belonged to a blanket. But what filled most of the box were drawings. One by one, he pulled out the faded papers, a smile tugging at his lips as familiar faces looked back at him. Of course, there were lots of Pooh. But there were also drawings of Eeyore, his expression grumpy. And little Piglet. There were pictures of Rabbit and Owl, and drawings of Tigger, Kanga, and Roo. With each picture, the memory of the Hundred-Acre Wood grew stronger, as did his memories of all the adventures he had gone on with his friends.

A grumble from Pooh startled Christopher. Shaken, Christopher dropped the picture he was looking at. It fluttered to the ground. Deciding it was well and truly time for bed, Christopher made his way over to the door. Turning off the light, he took one last look at his friend. "Good night, Winnie the Pooh," he whispered. *I've missed you*, he added silently.

Heading into his own room, Christopher climbed into bed and turned off the light. It had been a long day, and while he thought sleep might be impossible with all the thoughts running through his head, he was asleep before his head hit the pillow.

* * *

A loud rumble jolted Christopher awake. Rubbing at his eyes, blurry from sleep, he heard the rumble again, louder this time. *What is that?* he thought, trying to make sense of the noise. They weren't near any train lines. And he hadn't heard of any construction happening in the area. The rumble came again, even louder this time. If it hadn't been for the comfortable feeling of the mattress underneath him, Christopher would have thought he was back on the battlefield.

Christopher groaned as his vision cleared and he saw that the sound was not, in fact, coming from warplanes soaring above but rather from Winnie the Pooh. It seemed that in the middle of the night, the bear had climbed out of Madeline's bed and crawled right into his. The bear's face was smooshed against Christopher's shoulder.

Another loud rumble woke up the sleeping bear and he hopped up. Turning so that his bottom was now directly in Christopher's face, Pooh stretched. "Time to make myself hungry with my stoutness exercise," he announced. Clearly the change of scenery did not bother Pooh enough to upset his morning routine. "Up, down, up, down—" Each time he bent over, the bear's bottom would swing in front of Christopher and his belly would rumble.

"You're already hungry, Pooh?" Christopher said, trying to avoid a face full of bear bottom.

Pooh paused. Hearing his tummy rumble, he nodded. "Oh, yes," he agreed, hopping off the bed.

Christopher flopped back against the pillows and watched as the bear waddled out of the room and disappeared down the stairs. For one blissful moment, peace and quiet descended over the master bedroom.

CRASH!

Christopher jumped out of bed as another loud crashing sound emerged from downstairs. Not even bothering to tie his robe, he flew down the stairs and skidded into the kitchen. The source of the crash was immediately obvious. One of the kitchen's shelves had come crashing down off the wall. Tins and jars were strewn all over the floor. And standing in the middle of it all, looking as innocent as a newborn baby, was Pooh.

"Your ladder is broken," he said.

Christopher shook his head as he bent over and began picking up the mess Pooh had made. "It's not a ladder, Pooh," he said. "It *was* a shelf."

"That explains why it was no good for climbing," Pooh said, nodding.

"I don't have time to muck about," Christopher said, sighing. He dumped a few broken pieces of the glass jars into the garbage. "I should be working. Finding a solution." Then, more to himself than to the bear, he added, "Even though I think it may be impossible."

He then opened a jar of honey, which was a surprise find to Christopher, because he had thought the bear had eaten his entire supply the night before. Pooh shrugged. "People say Nothing is impossible," he said, stuffing his paw into the jar. "But I do Nothing every day."

"Oh, Pooh. That's not—oh, never mind," Christopher said, waving his hand. He knew it was useless to try and explain himself, or his motivations, to the bear, but he found himself doing it anyway. "Look, I'm an adult now. With responsibilities. I can't be distracted. Which is why we really need to get you home."

"But how?" Pooh asked.

Christopher felt a small pang of guilt. He realized that Pooh had come to him for help and that he was failing his old friend terribly. But he couldn't waste the weekend. He had specifically *not* gone away to be with his own family so that he *could* work. Getting caught up in Pooh's misadventures was a waste of time—plain and simple. Still . . . *perhaps* he should try to help.

CRASH!

Another shelf fell to the floor at that moment, dropping a sack of flour to the ground and sending a plume of white powder up into the air and all over Christopher. No. He had been right the first time. Picking Pooh up and putting him under his arm, Christopher began to head upstairs. He needed to get dressed. Then they were heading to Sussex, to get Pooh back to the Hundred-Acre Wood.

Chapter Five

OF course, getting a talking bear through the streets of London wasn't exactly easy. As Christopher hurried down the street—briefcase in one hand, Pooh under his other arm—he regretted not taking a cab to the train station. It seemed to Christopher that every person in London was out and about, enjoying the early morning sunshine. He had to duck and weave constantly. Grumbling under his breath, Christopher tried to bring as little attention to himself as possible.

Pooh, on the other hand, was doing the exact opposite.

"It's very loud," Pooh said, squirming. His head swiveled back and forth as he took in the speeding cars, the passing people, and the constant thrum of activity. "And not in a hummy sort of way," he added as a particularly loud and smelly double-decker bus blew by.

"Welcome to London," Christopher said.

Spotting a man approaching, Pooh waved. "Hello there," he called out. "Are you on an expotition, too?"

The man did a double take . . . and walked straight into a lamppost.

Wincing, Christopher slammed his hand over Pooh's mouth and then dove into one of London's many red phone booths. He plopped the bear onto the ledge that held the booth's phone and pointed a finger at his friend. "Look," he said, his tone serious. "People can't see you moving and talking."

"But why?" Pooh asked, looking genuinely confused. Christopher moved and talked to people. It seemed like that was what people in London did.

Christopher sighed. It felt like trying to reason with a toddler. He flashed back to when Madeline, age two, had constantly asked, "Why?" He had never been able to satisfy her questioning then, and he doubted he would be able to explain himself to Pooh now. But he had to try. He couldn't spend the rest of this "expotition," as Pooh called it, trying to hide the bear from view. "You're different," Christopher finally said. "And people don't like things that are different."

"Oh," Pooh said. "So, I shouldn't be me?"

"I . . . no . . . I . . ." Christopher stuttered. "No, always be yourself."

Pooh cocked his head. "This is all very confusing," the bear said. Then he patted his stomach. "It may be the hunger."

Christopher nearly laughed out loud. And he probably would have—if he hadn't been standing in a phone booth trying to reason with a bear and most likely getting strange looks from anyone who happened to pass by and look into the booth. "You've just eaten!" he said, exasperated.

"Oh! That's right," Pooh said, delighted to know he wasn't hungry. "I suspect, then, that I ate too much."

Christopher bit his tongue. They were wasting time. Which, of course, he hated. "Never mind that," he said. "Listen, for now, just maybe be a less exuberant you." The bear stared back at him blankly. "Flop. Sag. Go limp," Christopher said. As he spoke, he demonstrated. He flopped his head down, made his arms go limp. Then his whole body sagged so that he fell back against the booth's glass. On the other side, a person walking by jumped at the sound and then gave Christopher—and Pooh—a confused look before picking up the pace and moving on.

If this keeps up, Christopher thought as Pooh attempted to mimic his moves, *I'm going to have the whole city of London believing I've lost my mind.* He looked at Pooh. The bear had flopped his ears, hunched his shoulders, and gone bowlegged. Yet he still looked more like a real bear than a stuffed toy. And right then, Christopher needed him to look like a toy. Then he had a thought. "I've got it!" he cried. "Play nap time."

"Oh!" Pooh said, clapping his paws in delight. "I *love* play!" And just like that, Pooh went still. He looked exactly, Christopher thought happily, like a stuffed animal.

"Well done!" Christopher said, scooping him up and throwing him over his shoulder. Opening the phone booth, he stepped back onto the street and headed toward the entrance to Victoria station.

Luckily, they didn't have to go far, and Pooh managed to make it almost to the train before curiosity got the best of him. Opening one eye ever so slightly, Pooh looked around at the station. It didn't seem much different from the street. It was just darker and the sound was more muffled. He had started to close his eye when he spotted a balloon vendor. The man was holding a dozen or so brightly colored balloons, hawking them to passersby. Pooh's eyes shot open. There was nothing he liked more than a bright balloon.

"Oh!" he whispered into Christopher's ear. "May I please have a travel balloon?"

Christopher hushed his friend. "You don't need a balloon," he said, speaking out of the side of his mouth in such a way that he ended up resembling a bad ventriloquist.

"I know I don't *need* one," Pooh said. "But I would like one. Very, very much."

Sighing, Christopher made his way toward the

balloon vendor. If he had learned anything from being a parent, it was that sometimes saying yes saved everyone a whole lot of trouble. If Pooh was anything like Madeline when she was younger, saying no at this point could very well end in a tantrum of sorts. And in this case, it could end up with Pooh no longer wanting to play "nap time." That was something Christopher wanted to avoid very much. "One balloon, please," he said to the vendor.

"Color?" the man asked.

"Red!" Pooh said before Christopher could stop him. Luckily, the vendor's head was turned, so he didn't see that it was the bear, not the man, who had answered. Plucking a red balloon from the bunch, he handed it over to Christopher. Quickly, Christopher paid the man and headed toward the ticket counter. On his shoulder, Pooh clutched the balloon string and was back to looking like a stuffed toy (but one that now looked like a very happy and content stuffed toy).

Pleased that he had avoided garnering any unwanted attention, Christopher steadily made his way up to the ticket counter. "A return ticket, please," he requested, choosing to ignore the odd look the man behind the counter gave him as he placed Pooh, and the balloon, down on the ground so he could get his wallet. The balloon floated into his face and he batted it away. "To Hartfield, Sussex," he added. The balloon then settled back in front of his face. "Can I have some space please?" he hissed down in Pooh's direction. The balloon drifted a few feet back. Nodding, Christopher finished paying and took his ticket. Slipping it into his wallet, he glanced at his watch. They had made it.

"Two minutes to spare," Christopher noted. "Good, yes?"

There was no response.

Christopher's eyes shot to where Pooh *should* have been.

The bear—and the red balloon—were gone.

* * *

Pooh had been enjoying himself quite thoroughly. Doing as Christopher asked, he had given the man some space and was now wandering through the London train station, taking in the sights. The red balloon drifted lazily above him.

Spotting a young boy sitting in a stroller, Pooh wobbled over to say hello. Unfortunately, he hadn't anticipated how eager the boy would be to make a new friend. Or rather, take a new friend. The boy had grabbed Pooh, and the balloon, and dragged both into the stroller with him. While Pooh did enjoy getting a lift whenever possible, he was now beginning to get a bit nervous that he might not make it back to Christopher Robin.

"Mine!" the boy shouted as a large trolley of luggage was pushed past.

Pooh squirmed in the boy's death grip. "Are we going to be friends?" the bear asked. Because the tightening grip on his body was beginning to make him feel like that might not be the case.

Thankfully, just as Pooh was beginning to feel quite suffocated, Christopher rushed over. "He was mine first!" Christopher said, grabbing Pooh from the boy's grasp.

"That is true," Pooh said happily.

The boy, however, did not seem satisfied with this reasoning. Tilting back his head, he began to shriek.

Hearing the commotion, the boy's mother, who had been talking to a luggage porter, turned. Her eyes flitted back and forth between Christopher, who was clutching Pooh tightly to his chest, and her son, who was still screaming, arms reaching out for the bear. "Oh, for heaven's sake!" the mother said. "Did you take my son's toy?"

Christopher pulled Pooh closer. "You can't just steal teddy bears from grown men!" he snapped, instantly mortified by what he had said. Luckily, just then, a train whistle echoed through the station.

"Last call for boarding!" the conductor called out. "Last call!"

Sidestepping the boy's mother, who was now rather angry, as well as confused, Christopher hurtled toward the departing train's platform. The balloon floated behind him as he raced to catch the train. "You were *supposed* to be playing nap time," he muttered to Pooh as he ran.

"It was one of my smaller naps," Pooh answered. He was dangling upside down from Christopher's hand. His eyes widened, however, as he spotted a candy stand. Even upside down, the tasty treats looked delicious. As if sensing the bear's thoughts, Christopher's grip on Pooh's leg tightened and he sped up.

A moment later, Christopher threw himself into a train's carriage car. His chest heaved as he struggled to catch his breath. Behind him, the train doors closed with a bang. Christopher let out a sigh of relief. They had made it! Now he just needed to find a club car and keep Pooh hidden until they got out into the countryside.

But when Christopher tried to move forward, he couldn't. Upon looking over his shoulder, he let out a groan. The blasted balloon was *outside* of the train door—blowing around uncontrollably!

Noticing the problem at the same time, Pooh let out a shout. "Christopher Robin!" he said, pointing. In response, Christopher reached down and slipped the string off Pooh's paw. "But my balloon!" Pooh protested, watching it flutter wildly as the train picked up speed.

"It's gone now," Christopher said. "You don't need it."

Pooh frowned. "But it did make me very happy," he said softly. "Didn't it make you happy?"

Christopher began to walk down the narrow train aisle. "Not really," he said, too tired to pretend to be the boy he had once been. The man he was now was exhausted. Exhausted and exasperated! He just wanted to get to the country and get Pooh home.

Then his life could go back to normal.

Chapter Six

Christopher stared down at the pile of papers on the table in front of him. He had been working on them since the train pulled out of Victoria station nearly two hours ago, and he was no closer to coming up with a solution than he had been before. His sleeves were pushed up to his elbows, his hair was disheveled, and he was pained by numerous paper cuts from the small pieces of colored paper he had ripped up and taped sporadically across the equations as he agonized over finding numbers that would keep his staff intact.

Sighing, Christopher flipped over another piece of paper. This one had a list of employee's names typed on it. Looking over the list, he crossed off two names. In the margins, he wrote *17%* and circled the number.

His pen dug into the paper as he continued to circle the number over and over—and still over yet again. They weren't just names to him: he knew the two people he had just so callously crossed off. He knew their families, where they were from, what they liked to do for fun. He sighed again.

"Do you always have a case with you?"

Pooh's question jolted Christopher and forced him to refocus. He looked across the table at the bear. He had been sitting quietly—much to Christopher's surprise—since they had left London. He had spent most of the time staring out the window at the passing scenery.

"My briefcase?" Christopher clarified, pointing to the leather satchel propped open on the table. He nodded. "Most of the time, yes."

"Is it more important than a balloon?" Pooh asked.

"It's more important than a balloon, yes," Christopher answered. Apparently, the bear hadn't just been aimlessly staring out the window.

Pooh nodded. "I see," he said. "So, more like a blanket?"

Christopher bit back a groan. Once again, he found himself drawing a comparison between Pooh and Madeline as a younger child. The incessant questioning started off cute, but he knew it would quickly become a bit, well, monotonous. "Sure," he finally said after pondering Pooh's query. "More like a blanket." He hoped that in agreeing he might put an end to the conversation. He was wrong.

"What does it do?" Pooh asked, taking a closer look at the case.

"It holds very important things," Christopher said, shutting it with a *thwack* before Pooh's prying paws found their way inside. "Do you mind amusing yourself for a minute? I have work to do." Turning his attention back to his papers, he was surprised to find that Pooh seemingly had listened to him. For a moment, the train compartment was quiet.

And then it wasn't.

"House. Clouds. House. Grass," Pooh's voice broke the silence. "Dog. More grass."

Christopher sighed. "What are you doing?" he said,

looking back up at the bear. Pooh was staring out the window again.

"I'm playing a game," Pooh responded, not shifting his gaze. "It's called Say What You See."

"Well, can you play it a little quieter, please?" Christopher asked. Once again, he was surprised that Pooh seemed to listen and that it grew quiet. But once again, the peace and quiet didn't last.

"House. Tree. Grass." Pooh continued to list anything he saw through the train compartment's windows. He did, in his defense, do it a bit more quietly. "Tree. Pond. Tree. I don't know what that is. Bush. A man. House . . ."

A part of Christopher, the part that felt the beginnings of a serious headache forming, wanted to snap at Pooh and tell him to just not speak. But another part of him knew it wasn't worth it. The bear was just being who he was. And he *had* told Pooh that he should be himself, so it didn't seem right to fight it. With a sigh, he pinched the bridge of his nose. He was just going to have to hope that the bear grew tired of his game sooner rather than later.

Returning his attention to the papers in front of him, Christopher continued to run his calculations. He had at least another hour before they would reach Hartfield in Sussex. If he worked hard enough, he could make some headway . . . he hoped.

* * *

Fortunately, at least from Christopher's perspective, Pooh's game quickly tired the bear out and he fell asleep, leaving Christopher time to work uninterrupted. He sat, hunched over his papers, furiously scribbling and calculating. He ran and reran numbers and scenarios. He analyzed the data this way and that until he was sure his eyes were crossing. But by the time the train pulled into the station in Hartfield, there was a big red number twenty at the top of his papers.

He had done it. It was at a terrible cost to some, but he had done what his boss had asked. Now he just had to get back to London and deliver the news. But first he needed to get Pooh back to the Hundred-Acre Wood.

As the train let out a loud whistle and steam hissed from the engine car, Christopher picked up Pooh and put him over his shoulder. Grabbing the briefcase in his other hand, Christopher weaved his way back down the train car toward the door. To his surprise and Pooh's delight, the red balloon was still where it had been left, its string wedged between the door and the train car's side. Grabbing the string, Pooh let out a happy shout. Christopher barely registered it.

The drive from the station had always felt like forever to Christopher when he was younger. The anticipation of getting to the house and out into the woods had made the minutes pass as slowly as hours. Back then, he had barely registered the passing countryside or the lovely homes that lined the way. There was only one house he wanted to see, only one wood he wanted to register.

Oddly enough, he found now, as the taxi meandered down the country roads, that he felt nearly the same way. His foot tapped against the floor and his knee bounced up and down. It had been years since he had visited the family country house. He couldn't help wondering what it would look like. Would it feel as big? Would the trees seem smaller? Had it aged the same way he had . . . ?

The taxi turned down the drive, and Christopher's heart began to beat faster. The trees on either side had grown tall and thick in his absence and now reached over the drive, making it feel as though they were passing through a tunnel. Then, up ahead, Christopher saw a burst of light and the house came into view.

Christopher's breath caught. The house hadn't changed. It was still stately and comfortable at the same time. The grounds were still manicured and the paint seemed fresh. If Christopher hadn't known better, he would have sworn that not a day had passed since he and his mother had visited the home after his father's death all those years ago.

For a long moment he sat motionless in the back of the taxi. He knew he needed to get out, but a part of him didn't want to step outside and possibly ruin the illusion. He knew that things up close tended to look different than when viewed from afar. The house could be falling apart inside, or small cracks in the paint might be visible for all he knew. In the back of the cab, he could fool himself for a little while longer. But finally, with a sigh, he grabbed Pooh and the briefcase, paid the driver, and stepped out into the country air.

Looking up at the far-right window, he saw that the curtain had been pulled shut. Evelyn must have been using his parents' old room while she was there. Hoping that the sound of the departing taxi wouldn't alert her, Christopher quickly ducked around the side of the house.

"Are we going in?" Pooh asked, pointing at the house as they made their way toward the backyard.

Christopher put a finger to his lips and shook his head. "No," he whispered. "No, we must keep very quiet. Not let them see us." Passing under a window, Christopher ducked down. He motioned for Pooh to do the same. "Stay low," he added.

Despite the warning, Pooh continued to walk normally. Unlike Christopher, the bear was small enough to pass right under the window unseen. But just because someone looking out couldn't see him, that didn't mean he didn't want to see *in.* Stopping at the next window, Pooh lifted himself up onto the tips of his paws and peered through the glass. "Who's that?" he asked.

Whipping around, Christopher bit back a shout. "Pooh!" he hissed.

"She can't be Pooh," the bear said, confusing the warning with an answer. "*I'm* Pooh."

Making his way back to the window, Christopher carefully peeked over the windowsill and into the room beyond. Evelyn was in the family room, arranging a bouquet of bright flowers in a vase. "That's Evelyn. My wife," he said softly. While he had just seen her a day ago, she somehow looked different. Happier, maybe? Or more content?

"She looks very kind," Pooh observed.

"She is," Christopher said, his gaze lingering on Evelyn as Pooh wandered to the next window.

"And who is she?" Pooh asked.

Christopher snapped to attention. Pooh had managed to pull himself up so that nearly half his body was above the windowsill, clearly visible to whomever was inside. Ducking back down, Christopher awkwardly hunched his way over and pulled the bear back down. But as he did so, he caught sight of his daughter, sitting in a chair far too large for her, surrounded by textbooks. Her expression was serious, her eyebrows furrowed in concentration as she tried to make sense of the book on her lap. "That's Madeline," he told Pooh. "My daughter."

Pooh's expression brightened. "Can she come play with us?" he asked innocently.

Shaking his head, Christopher moved away from the window so he could stand up straight. "No," he answered. "She can't come." They weren't, he wanted to point out, "playing." But arguing semantics with Pooh seemed a colossal waste of time, so instead he kept walking toward the back of the house. Pooh followed.

"Do you not like playing with her?" Pooh asked as they walked.

"No," Christopher said. "But she's very busy working right now."

Pooh nodded. Then he stopped. He looked down at the case Christopher still had clutched in his hand, then back at the house. "Does she have a briefcase like you?"

"No!" Christopher snapped, the response laced with more venom then he intended. Yes, his daughter was studious. No, they didn't play all the time. But did that mean she wasn't a normal kid? No! It most certainly did not. Taking a breath, Christopher quieted his inner rant. He knew he was being sensitive, but what did Pooh know about the real world anyway?

As if to prove his point, Pooh held out his balloon. "Do you think she'd like my red balloon?" he asked. "It might make her happy."

Once more, Christopher's temper flared. This time, he didn't hold his thoughts inside. "What is it with you and the balloon?" he snapped angrily. "Happiness isn't just in balloons. Madeline *is* happy. And I'm happy she's happy. Now come on, Pooh." But even as he spoke the words, Christopher knew it wasn't Pooh he was trying to convince. It was himself.

Luckily, Christopher was saved from conducting further introspection by their arrival at the edge of the woods. The trees created a natural fence of sorts for the Robins' country house, their thick branches reaching out over the manicured lawn. In the summer, those branches provided shade for picnics, and in the fall they blanketed the ground in brightly colored leaves. Christopher used to think of the area between the house and woods as magical—the place where anything became possible. Disappearing into the woods as a child, Christopher could leave behind his worries and his fears and become the adventurous friend and hero he always wanted to be.

Staring into the woods now, he was overcome with the same feeling of anticipation that he would get when he was a boy, just before he let the trees engulf him. Only now there was a nervous and anxious energy to the anticipation he was feeling. Taking a deep breath, he plunged his way into the woods. Pooh followed. The path he had used to take was overgrown now, but he could still make it out under the decades' worth of decayed leaves. He smiled sadly. Even this place couldn't be saved from the effects of time.

Neither bear nor man spoke much as they made their way deeper into the woods. Lost in their own thoughts, they watched as the sun filtered through the branches overhead, dappling the forest floor with light. Birds sang out and animals rustled among the leaves. It was peaceful—and for just a moment, Christopher felt some of the weight on his shoulders lift.

And then they arrived at the old tree with the hollowed-out trunk. While everything else seemed bigger and older—and more weatherworn, to Christopher—the tree appeared unchanged. The bark was still the same rough grey, and his initials, carved into the tree's side so many years ago, were still there. The *C* and *R* sported a blocky and childish appearance. Reaching out, Christopher ran his hand over the bark fondly. Then he sighed. "Well, Pooh," he said, turning to his friend, "I got you home."

Pooh cocked his head. "Aren't you coming with me?" he asked.

"I can't," Christopher said. "I have to get back to London."

"But I need your help," Pooh protested. "I have lost all of my friends." He looked up at Christopher. He really didn't understand this new version of his old friend. His old friend would never have left him alone. His old friend would have loved the red balloon. His old friend would have been excited to go on an adventure. This new Christopher was no fun at all. Pooh sighed. He missed his old friend Christopher Robin.

Ignoring the sigh, Christopher shrugged. "Perhaps they're back now," he said, though he knew he didn't sound very convincing. "And you can tell them all about your adventures."

"I would like to do that," Pooh said, nodding.

"Then off you go!" Christopher said.

Pooh hesitated for a moment. He wanted to say more, perhaps change Christopher's mind, but the man was already looking at his watch and tapping his foot in anticipation of leaving. So instead, Pooh wrapped his arms around Christopher's legs and hugged him. Hard. "Good-bye, Christopher Robin!" he said, squeezing even tighter.

The gesture caught Christopher off guard. Awkwardly, he reached down and patted Pooh on the back. "Good-bye, Pooh," he said. Then he nudged him toward the hole in the tree's trunk, his beloved red balloon trailing behind him.

Without another word, Pooh ducked down and disappeared inside. Christopher let out a sigh of relief, his duty done. Now he could get back to the city and focus on his work. But as he turned to go, he caught sight of Pooh's red balloon. It was floating in the entry to the door.

Moving down, he peered inside the large hole in the base of the tree. Pooh was in front of the green door that Christopher had always used to enter their special spot in the Hundred-Acre Wood. The bear was just crouched down, not moving.

"What are you doing, Pooh?" Christopher asked,

confused. He would have thought the bear would have been eager to get through the door and back home.

Pooh looked over his shoulder at Christopher. "Sometimes if I am going Somewhere and I wait, Somewhere comes to me."

"Right," Christopher said, trying to wrap his head around the bear's somewhat cryptic response. Then he let out another sigh. He really didn't have time to dilly-dally. He had to get back to the station and catch the next train home to London. He pushed himself back so he was once again in the opening of the tree trunk. "Well, good luck with everything." He knew that that was a terribly unhelpful thing to say, but it was all he could think of.

Pooh didn't bother to even look at him when he responded. "I will need good luck," he said, the answer sounding even sadder in the hollowed-out tree trunk, "for I am a Bear of Very Little Brain."

"Yes, um," Christopher stammered, not sure what to say to that. "Well, good-bye," he finally said again and crawled completely out of the tree. As he stood up, he hit the red balloon, which was still floating near the door. He shoved it into the hole. Once more, he started to walk away. And once more, he couldn't help pausing to look over his shoulder.

The red balloon was still floating in the air in front of the entrance to the green door. Pooh still hadn't gone through.

Guilt enveloped Christopher. He knew that if he were to leave now, Winnie the Pooh would just sit there. And sit there. And sit there some more, hoping that "Somewhere" would come to him. But Christopher knew that would never happen. And he couldn't just leave the bear there. Pooh was his friend. He had tracked him down all the way in London. He needed his help. Christopher took a deep breath. Work would have to wait. Right now he had a friend who needed to get home, and he wasn't going to abandon him. Not again. Christopher hoisted his briefcase and put it under his arm. "Look out, Pooh!" he said, ducking back into the tree. "Here I come!"

Christopher Robin was going back to the Hundred-Acre Wood.

Chapter Seven

There was, however, just one problem with Christopher's plan to return to the Hundred-Acre Wood. And that problem was the green door inside the hollowed-out tree. For while the green door was the same green door it had been when Christopher last used it, Christopher was *not* the same. He was no longer a thin little boy with narrow shoulders and hips. He was a grown man with broad shoulders and a bit of a belly.

Which was why he now found himself stuck quite firmly in the middle of the door. His bottom half was on one side and his top half was on the other. It was, he couldn't help thinking, a position Pooh had often found himself in.

Pooh, who had gone through the green door first, turned and eyed his friend. He took in Christopher's top half and peered around to see where his bottom half was. Noting it was missing, he cocked his head. "Are you stuck?" he asked.

"Apparently, I am," Christopher said, his voice strained as the door squeezed his sides painfully.

"Happens to me all the time," Pooh said with a shrug. "Did you just eat honey?"

Christopher shook his head. "No. I did not just eat honey."

Taking a deep breath, he braced his arms back against the tree and pushed—hard. He didn't budge. He took another breath and pushed again. Still, he did not budge. Finally, sucking in as hard as he could, Christopher pushed one final time. With a *pop!* his body came loose of the doorway and he tumbled to his freedom.

He straightened up, stretching his arms toward the sky and then wincing. He was going to have some bruises. Bringing his hand to his head, he felt the hair sticking up and knew, without needing to look in a mirror, that he was in a rather disheveled state. He sighed.

At least he knew the chances of running into anyone from work here were nonexistent.

Distracted by his escape from the door, Christopher hadn't taken a moment yet to look around the woods. But now he did. And he was shocked by what he saw. Thick fog covered everything, and he shuddered as a chill swept over him. This was *not* the idyllic Hundred-Acre Wood he remembered. "Pooh?" he asked, turning to look at the bear. "Was it always this gloomy?"

"Yes," Pooh answered. Then he paused. "Or no. I forget which."

Christopher narrowed his eyes. He was rather certain that this was not how things had always been. He knew, in fact, that when he had come to the Hundred-Acre Wood as a child, it was never gloomy and only rarely even rainy. Since it hadn't always been like this, when had it changed? And why? A piece of him knew the answer but refused to acknowledge it. Instead, he returned his attention to the reason he was there now. "Well," he asked Pooh, "which way?"

"I was hoping you would know," Pooh answered.

Christopher shook his head. "I haven't been here in years," he pointed out. "How would I know?"

"Because you're Christopher Robin."

Pooh's response was so simple and so direct that Christopher couldn't even come up with a retort. The bear was looking up at him with complete trust. He didn't have any doubt that, somehow, Christopher would save the day. Looking at the bear looking at him, Christopher wished with a sudden ferocity that he could have such faith in himself. "Right," he said, putting on a brave face. "Yes, well, we need to follow this systematically."

Pooh, however, was only half listening. His attention had been caught by a bee that chose that moment to buzz by. "Follow this simple honey bee, yes." He began to wander off after the bee.

Pulling him back, Christopher shook his head. "No, Pooh. The key is to head in one direction, so as not to get lost." He gestured to the woods around them. "Especially in a fog like this." He tried to peer through the thick mist in the hopes of seeing a path or a sign.

Unfortunately, the fog had made everything take on the same ghostly and blurry appearance. There was no way to tell which way was which—not without some form of help.

Luckily, Christopher was always prepared.

Reaching into his pocket, he pulled out a small, round brass object. It was his compass. "From the war," he explained to Pooh, when the bear asked what it was and why he had it. "I still keep it with me." He moved it between his fingers in a rhythmic and practiced motion. The metal felt cool to the touch, the cover of the compass dinged and worn.

"What is a *war*?" Pooh asked.

"It's something we don't speak of," Christopher answered, leaving no room for discussion.

Just then, a clap of thunder echoed through the woods. Pooh looked down at his belly. "It would seem I am hungrier than I have ever been before."

Pleased to have a distraction—even one as unpleasant as thunder—Christopher looked up at the darkening sky. "It seems the weather is getting worse," he said.

Glancing back down at the compass, he watched the needle wobble. He wasn't sure what direction they were supposed to be going, but he figured that if they went north, and kept going in that direction, they couldn't get too terribly lost.

Unfortunately, while Christopher was staring at the compass, Pooh had been staring at him . . . and the compass contraption. It was the same color as honey, so he instantly liked it. Plus, Christopher had said it would help them get to where they were going. Something he also liked. The only problem he could see was that Christopher didn't seem ready to use it. So, he decided, after waddling over to his friend, he would just have to do it. "May I see the compass?" Pooh asked, holding out his paw.

Startled, Christopher handed it over.

Immediately, he regretted his actions.

Pooh began to walk away, compass in hand. "No! Wait!" Christopher shouted. "You must keep us north! North!" The words echoed back at him through the fog. Already, Pooh was disappearing from view.

"I'll follow the very handy arrow," Pooh shouted back over his shoulder.

Christopher let out a sigh. He had no choice but to follow Pooh—whatever direction that happened to be.

* * *

Pooh was getting worried. They had been walking for what felt like hours and hours, and they still hadn't seen any sign of his friends. They hadn't seen much, actually, except for a pervading fog. To help pass the time, Pooh had begun to play a little game as they walked. He tried to see shapes in the fog, the same way he would when he lay on his back and looked up at clouds in the sky. So far, he had made out a pot of honey. And a honey bee. And some honeycombs.

"Does anything look familiar?"

Christopher's question startled Pooh. He was tempted to ask if Christopher meant the pot of honey Pooh currently saw floating in the air beside Christopher's head, but he decided against it. "The fog?" he said instead.

"Besides the fog!" Christopher said, his tone impatient.

Just then, out of the fog, emerged something *other* than fog. Unfortunately, it was not something that Pooh was happy to see. It was a sign. And written on the sign, in childish handwriting, were these words: BEWARE OF HEFFALUMPS AND WOOZLES.

"Oh, bother," Pooh said, stopping short, leading Christopher to bump right into him.

"What's the matter?" Christopher asked. But upon peering around the bear to see the cause of his sudden stopping, he saw the sign. Recognizing the handwriting and the warning, he groaned. "You can't be serious. There are no such things as Heffalumps and Woozles."

Pooh pointed at the warning. "Of course there are," he said. "Didn't you see the sign?"

"Terrifying elephant- and weasellike beasts who wander the world to prey on happiness aren't real, Pooh," Christopher said. "Now come on." Pushing past the bear, Christopher walked right past the sign and continued on his way.

Watching him go, Pooh hesitated. He trusted Christopher Robin. He always had. But it had been Christopher Robin who'd helped paint the sign in the first place. So what was he to do? *I shall continue to do Nothing different*, Pooh decided, *for that is the best Something to do.* With his mind made up, he resumed walking.

"Christopher Robin," he said as they made their way through still more fog, "what is your work?" He wasn't entirely sure what "work" was, but Christopher mentioned it often enough that Pooh figured it was important.

"I'm an efficiency manager at a luggage company," Christopher answered.

Pooh nodded, though the words meant little to him. "Do you have many friends there?"

"I have people who rely on me," Christopher answered. Turning, he looked back at Pooh, curious why the bear was suddenly so interested in his life outside the Hundred-Acre Wood.

"So, yes," Pooh said.

He looked so pleased to think that Christopher had friends that the man suddenly found himself over-explaining himself and his role. "No," he said, shaking his head. "I don't think of them as friends. It only makes it harder if I have to let some of them go."

Pooh cocked his head. "Where will they go?" he asked, confusion written all over his innocent face and in his response.

"I don't know, Pooh," Christopher said. "I don't know." He swung his hand through the thick fog, as though trying to hit it. He *didn't* know. He had absolutely no idea what would happen to all the people who he had crossed off lists to make that magical 20 percent cut. He didn't know what would happen to their families. He didn't know if they would find other work. He had no idea about any of it, and up until now, he had been able to push the horrible, wracking guilt out of his mind. But now Pooh was making him see what he would truly be doing.

"Did you let *me* go?"

The bear's question bounced off the fog and echoed

in Christopher's head. He had never thought about it, but now, looking at the bear who still trusted him enough to follow him through the fog and believe his stories about Heffalumps and Woozles, Christopher came face-to-face with the realization that he hadn't been the only one to suffer when he went away to school. He had left the Hundred-Acre Wood and his friends; and yes, he had ultimately let Pooh go. He had let him go—and the result? He looked around at the gloomy woods. The result was a world gone to pieces.

He could only imagine what the world would look like for all the men and women who wouldn't have jobs by the following week's end. . . .

CHAPTER EIGHT

"Pooh? I swear that's the same sign."

Christopher was standing still in front of a sign that looked strangely like the one he and the bear had passed several hours ago. In the same childish writing was the warning to watch for Heffalumps and Woozles. Christopher peered closer. Then he groaned. It wasn't just strangely similar, it was *exactly* similar. It was the same sign. Looking over at Pooh, he narrowed his eyes. "Are you sure we're still headed north?"

"Let me look," Pooh replied, flipping open the compass.

"You haven't been looking?" Christopher said, a bad feeling forming in the pit of his stomach.

The bear shrugged. "Not since I started following

these footsteps." He pointed down at the ground in front of him.

Following his gaze, Christopher bit back a roar of frustration. "Pooh!" he said forcefully when he had managed to compose himself—just barely. "Those are *our* footsteps! We just went in a circle. What's wrong with you? All you had to do was follow the compass!" Even as he said the words, a part of Christopher knew he was being unfair. Pooh wasn't a weathered war vet. He wasn't even human. He was a bear!

Pooh's shoulders drooped and his ears went back. "But . . . the compass led us to the Heffalumps and Woozles," he said.

"There are no Heffalumps and Woozles!" Christopher responded, unmoved by Pooh's explanation. "I should never have trusted you with the compass."

"I'm sorry," Pooh said, his voice barely a whisper. "I'll put it back with the other Important Things." Walking over to Christopher, who was clutching the briefcase in his hands so hard that his knuckles had turned white, Pooh popped open the lock. Before Christopher could even blink, the briefcase fell open—and so did the brown folder full of all his paperwork. At the very same moment, a gust of wind blew through the woods, sending the "Important Things" flying.

Christopher let out a shout and began chasing after the loose papers. "They're irreplaceable! I'll never remember all of this!" he said as he bent and stretched, trying—but failing—to collect every sheet. As he pried one sheet of paper off a pricker bush, he looked over at Pooh. The bear was standing very still. For some reason, that made Christopher even more irate. Before he could stop himself, Christopher stalked over to the bear. Mean, angry words spewed from his mouth. "You know what? You're right, Pooh. You *are* a Bear of Very Little Brain. Do you know what will happen to me if I lose a single sheet of this? Winslow'll eat me for breakfast."

"A Woozle will eat you for breakfast?" Pooh said, incorrectly repeating what he thought Christopher had just said.

"Yes, Pooh," Christopher said, his voice quivering

and his eyes going wide and looking a bit crazy. "A big Woozle is going to gobble me up!"

Pooh, still not quite sure what to make of the scene unfolding in front of him, frowned. Christopher was laughing, but he didn't sound happy. And he was agreeing with Pooh, though he didn't seem to mean it. "That doesn't sound like fun," Pooh finally said.

Once more, Christopher let out the strange laugh that bothered Pooh. "It won't be," he agreed. "But *that's* the real world for you. There's more to life than balloons and honey, you silly bear. Why did you even come back?" He looked down at the papers in his hands, wet and limp from the heavy fog. His voice grew lower and his shoulders sagged. "I'm not a child. I'm an adult now. With adult responsibilities."

"But you're Christopher Robin," Pooh said.

"No, I'm not," Christopher said. "I'm not how you remember me."

Pooh shook his head. His friend *wasn't* how he remembered him, but he knew it was still Christopher Robin on the inside. He had just lost his way. He was foggy, like the Hundred-Acre Wood. From the sounds of it, though, Christopher didn't want to remember who he had been. "I'm sorry," Pooh said as he slowly began to back up. "You should let me go. For a *fish in the sea*."

"A fish in the–?" Christopher repeated, trying to figure out what Pooh meant. Then he realized it. "It's *efficiency*!" Stuffing the papers he had gathered back into the briefcase, he slammed it shut. When he looked up, Pooh was gone. The only thing Christopher could see was the fog still surrounding him.

Christopher gulped as silence fell over the woods. What had he just done?

* * *

As he ran through the foggy woods, Christopher's mind raced with unwanted thoughts. Thoughts of Pooh, lost and hungry. Thoughts of the bear, sad and alone. Over and over again a picture of Pooh's face, his eyes full of tears, flashed in front of Christopher, filling him with guilt. He hadn't meant to be so hard on Pooh. If he was being honest with himself, he had said all those things because he was mad at himself, not because of anything the bear had said. He was mad at himself for making the numbers "work" at the cost of peoples' jobs. He was mad at himself for having no choice but to do what his boss had said to do. He was mad at having to be efficient without feeling. And so he had yelled at Pooh, and Pooh, in turn, had disappeared.

And it was all his fault.

"Pooh!" he shouted. "Pooh! Where are you?" Over and over again he called into the fog, and over and over again the only response he got was his own voice echoing back to him. It was growing darker as the daylight hours faded. Christopher knew that if he didn't find Pooh soon, he would have to wait until the next day.

Christopher tripped over an unseen branch on the path in front of him, and his arm windmilled as he struggled to keep his balance. He managed to stay upright, but as he stopped to catch his breath, he found himself once more staring at the Heffalump warning sign. He had done the same thing Pooh had done: gone around in a complete circle. Only this time, instead of staying away from the sign, Christopher ran straight toward it. "There are no Heffalumps!" he said to the air. Then, with a burst of speed, he brushed past the sign and headed right in the direction the sign warned him *not* to go.

He ran and ran until the sun sank behind the trees, throwing the woods into an early dusk. Shadows that had been harmless in the day became frightening as they lengthened. The rustling of the trees, once simple white noise, now sounded eerie, causing Christopher to move faster. His eyes scanned the darkening woods, desperately seeking any sign of Pooh. He saw nothing.

But then he heard something. A roar filled the woods. It was a horrifying noise that was a cross between what an elephant and a dinosaur would sound like. Christopher stopped in his tracks; the hair on his arms stood on end. It couldn't be. Could it? "Heffalumps and Woozles are not real," he said, hoping to reassure himself. He moved forward, his eyes now scanning the woods for not just Pooh, but creatures he hoped against hope didn't exist.

And then he heard that very same roar again.

Christopher spun around, his head swiveling left and right—then right and left. "Not real, not real, not real," he chanted. But as he did so, the fog began to lift, and through it, Christopher saw shadows appear. Large shadows that looked a lot like elephants. Or more precisely, a herd of Heffalumps.

Another roar sounded. This time, Christopher didn't hesitate. He turned and ran . . .

Right into a Heffalump trap!

With a shout, Christopher felt his legs go out from underneath him—and then he was falling through the air. He landed with a *thump* at the bottom of a large hole. "Ouch," he said. Lying on the cold ground, he caught his breath. He could hear the Heffalumps roaring and was, for the moment, pleased to be ten feet below ground and not any place where they could see him.

When he felt he had lain there long enough, Christopher pushed himself to his feet. He craned his head back, looking way up to the opening of the hole above him. He could see the first stars glinting in the sky above. He knew soon enough he wouldn't be able to see his own hands, let alone the top of the hole. He had to get out of there—fast.

Turning, he scanned the area. To his surprise and annoyance, the first thing he saw was a sign that read: HEFFALUMP TRAP—GOTCHA! He groaned. "But I'm not a Heffalump," he said softly. Then, his voice growing louder, he began to shout. "They're out there! I'm down here!" But no one answered his call. There was no one who could hear him. Except perhaps the Heffalumps. "You are talking to no one," he said. *First I lose Pooh. Then I run into imaginary creatures who are not imaginary and end up falling in a silly trap that was supposed to catch the imaginary creatures. Truly, could it get any worse?*

And then, as if Mother Nature were listening, it began to rain.

The drops fell slowly at first but then grew larger and fell faster. It didn't take long for the ground beneath his feet to grow muddy. Christopher felt a fresh wave of panic wash over him. He had to get out of there.

Frantically, he began to try to climb. His fingers dug into the crumbling dirt that made up the hole's walls. But he couldn't get any purchase. His fingers would just slip and he would come away with nothing but a handful of mud. Over and over again he tried. But always, the results were the same. It didn't matter which side he attempted to climb or how he attempted to climb up; he just kept falling. And then, just when he thought all hope was lost, he began to inch ever so slowly up. One foot, then two, then three. The hole's edge appeared, almost within reach. Christopher reached up, his fingers grasping for the edge at the top. He felt a fresh wave of air hit his face and then—

He lost his grip and went tumbling backward.

With another thud, he once more found himself on the floor of the hole. *"Noooooo!"* he shouted. *"Heeelllp!"*

As if in answer, the rain began to fall even harder. The hole was filling up with water. It was at Christopher's shins already and didn't show any signs of stopping. Looking around for anything that could help him, Christopher spotted a vine dangling from the top of the hole. Putting down his briefcase, which made him realize that may have been part of what was impeding his escape, Christopher grabbed his umbrella from between the case's handles. Then, standing on top of the briefcase, he reached up, stretching the handle of the umbrella toward the vine until it just ever so slightly seemed to hook on.

YANK!

Christopher pulled down hard on the vine. Nothing happened. He yanked again. Still nothing. Then he did it again.

This time, something did happen. Unfortunately, it was not what Christopher had hoped. Instead of yanking the vine down, Christopher managed to dislodge a rock. The rock, and the vine, came tumbling down into the hole. Before he could duck out of the way, the rock slammed into the top of Christopher's head.

The last thing Christopher saw before he crumpled to the ground, unconscious, was a gush of water that came pouring down the side of the hole.

Chapter Nine

"Owwww. Ow. Ow. Ow."

The pain in Christopher's head jolted him awake. Gingerly, he reached up and ran his fingers over the top of his head. A large bump was already forming—and even the most tentative of touches sent a shot of pain streaking all the way down to his toes. He let out another groan, but it turned into a yelp when Christopher realized the water had risen while he had been unconscious. It was now all the way up to his chest.

"Pooh!" Christopher shouted, panic filling him. "Pooh!" He didn't want to be stuck in a hole in the middle of the Hundred-Acre Wood. He needed to see Evelyn. And Madeline. He needed to tell them how much he loved them and how sorry he was and how much . . .

"Hello, Christopher Robin!"

Looking up, Christopher nearly wept when he saw Pooh peering down at him from the top of the hole. The bear's familiar face was the best thing Christopher had seen in a long, long time. "Oh, thank goodness, you're all right," he said. "Can you help me?" he added as the water level rose.

"Of course," Pooh answered.

Nodding, Christopher began to look around to see how they could make this work. "Okay," he said, "I think I can get some leverage if you could just pass me a rope or—"

SPLASH!

The sound of a rather large object hitting the water next to him startled Christopher Robin and he let out a shout. A moment later, Pooh popped up from beneath the surface and began treading water beside him. The bear seemed completely unafraid of the fact that he was now swimming in a hole that was designed to catch Heffalumps. He looked over at Christopher and gave him a smile.

"What did you do that for?" Christopher asked, dumbfounded.

"You seemed lonely down here," Pooh answered.

"But now we're *both* stuck," Christopher said, his voice coming uncomfortably close to a whine. "And there are Heffalumps and Woozles out there. We're not safe at all." Just then, his briefcase floated by. Reaching out, Christopher grabbed it. Then he grabbed Pooh and tried to get him on top of it. If they both had to be trapped, the least he could do was protect Pooh. "We must get out of here. But I'm not sure what to do anymore."

Pooh, who had not complained when Christopher grabbed him and shoved him onto the briefcase, looked down at him. His eyes were calm, and he did not seem to notice the water splashing up and over him, soaking his fur. "Sometimes the thing to do is Nothing," he finally said with a shrug.

In the water beside him, Christopher stopped struggling. "Nothing?" he repeated.

Pooh nodded. "It often leads to the best Something."

As the bear spoke, the briefcase beneath him shifted in the moving water, throwing him off-balance. Pooh slipped off the briefcase and sank under the water. Within moments, all that could be seen of the bear was a trail of bubbles that rose to the surface.

Oddly enough, Christopher didn't feel a sense of panic as he watched the bear disappear. Instead, he felt eerily calm. There was a dreamy quality to everything. The water didn't even feel cold as it rose higher and higher up his chest. He wondered if he was actually drowning. He had heard that people who drowned often just slipped into unconsciousness. Maybe that was what was happening to him. He stopped treading water and let himself sink.

Down, down, down he went until his backside touched the bottom of the hole. Looking over, he saw Pooh calmly sitting on the ground. He was breathing normally, and when he spoke, the words did not gurgle the way one would expect if one were listening to someone else speak underwater. "It's quite nice, isn't it?" Pooh asked.

"Yes, quite nice," Christopher said. But he was beginning to think that it was all a bit too nice. Something was not right. Then he glanced down at his hands. Or rather, where his hands *had* been. They had been transformed into Heffalump hands. And when he reached up to touch his ears, he realized they were the large, floppy ears of a Heffalump. His eyes growing wide, he turned to Pooh for help, but the frightened bear frantically began to try to swim away from him.

Desperately, Christopher reached out to comfort his friend, but instead of his arm, a large trunk moved through the water. It extended toward Pooh and then, before Christopher knew what was happening, the trunk sucked Pooh up.

Christopher started spinning around and around. He had to get out of this hole. But every time he spun around, he came face-to-face with another Heffalump: a Heffalump version of himself. He couldn't escape the creature. He couldn't escape himself. As he spun faster and faster, he felt as though the air was being sucked from his lungs, and then one of the other Heffalumps' trunks connected to him. He felt a strong pull and then, just like Pooh, he was sucked into the creature's trunk. . . .

* * *

Christopher woke with a gasp. His breath heaved in his chest and he felt his heart pounding. It had been a dream! There were no Heffalumps. No powerful trunks. He was alive!

But, as he took stock of his actual situation, he realized he wasn't much better off. While he had been unconscious, the water *had* risen. He had managed to stay afloat by clinging to the briefcase, just like Pooh had been doing in his dream. It had acted like a life preserver. But the rain was still falling and Christopher knew he needed to quickly find a way out of the hole.

Just then, his hands slipped on the briefcase and he slid into the water. He flashed back to his dream and felt the panic he should have felt then start to fill him. But before panic overwhelmed him, Christopher felt his feet hit the bottom. Pushing back up, he burst through the surface of the water with a triumphant cry. The water was *filling* the hole. So, if he just waited . . .

"Just do Nothing," Christopher said, echoing Pooh's words.

Floating onto his back, Christopher let his arms spread out and his legs lift up. Underneath him, his overcoat billowed out so that from above, he looked like he was lying on a beige raft. And then, he just did "Nothing." He did Nothing as the rain continued to fall and the water in the hole rose higher and higher. He did Nothing as the sky began to brighten and the stars began to fade. He did absolutely Nothing until, finally, he could do Something.

When the water neared the top of the hole, he flipped onto his front and swam to the edge. He then pulled himself up onto the surrounding solid ground and collapsed. He lay there for a long moment, enjoying the feel of the dirt beneath him—and the steadiness of the ground. When he had caught his breath, he turned back to the hole, fished out his briefcase and umbrella, and stood up.

He was out of the trap. He was free.

Now he needed to go find Pooh.

Taking off into the woods, Christopher shouted out the names of his friends. "Pooh? Eeyore?" he called. "Anyone?" No answer came, but still he kept going. The woods weren't *that* big. He had to run into someone eventually.

And then, just like that, he saw something he recognized. Slowing, he grinned as Pooh Sticks Bridge came into view. He moved closer. Christopher's grin grew wider. Sure enough, there was a sign that read: POOH STIX. One side was labeled DROPING SID, and the other was labeled WATCHIN SID. He couldn't remember the number of times he and Pooh had come here to play their made-up game. It was so simple and silly—dropping a stick from one side of the bridge and running to the other to watch it appear—but it had entertained them for hours upon hours.

Walking onto the bridge, Christopher looked over the railing on the "dropping side." His reflection stared back at him. But the person looking up at him wasn't a young boy full of innocence. The face that stared back at him was old. Old and caked in drying grey mud. Frowning, Christopher picked up a stick at his feet and threw it down, shattering the reflection. Then, out of habit, he stepped to the opposite side of the bridge to watch his stick float by.

But instead of a stick, he saw Eeyore. The pessimistic donkey floated out from under the bridge. He was on his back, staring up at the sky with a frown of his own. Upon seeing Christopher, the dour look only deepened. "Just my luck," he said in his sad voice. "A Heffalump. Leering at his lunch."

"Eeyore!" Christopher shouted happily. "I'm not a Heffalump!" He was so glad he had finally found one of his friends that he wasn't even upset he had been mistaken for an elephant-like creature.

The donkey shrugged. "Doesn't matter anyway," he said. "Headed for the waterfall. Be gone soon."

Turning, Christopher looked in the direction Eeyore was floating. Sure enough, there was a waterfall. "Swim! Swim!" he shouted to the donkey.

But Eeyore made no attempt to swim. Instead, he somehow managed to start floating faster. As Christopher watched, the donkey's body disappeared briefly as it dipped down one of the smaller falls leading to the larger one. The water turned rougher as Eeyore entered the faster-moving part of the stream. He was getting closer and closer to the large waterfall. If Christopher didn't do something, he would lose another friend before he had even really found him.

Racing off the bridge, Christopher began to run along the shore, calling out to Eeyore as he did.

"Maybe it's for the best," Eeyore responded, his voice monotone despite the dire circumstances he was facing. "Can't change the inevitable. Just have to go with the flow."

Approaching a spot on the shore that jutted out into the water, Christopher slipped and slid down until his toes touched the stream. He reached out his hand as Eeyore floated past. But it was no use. The donkey was too far out and his arms weren't long enough. "Don't worry, Eeyore!" he shouted.

"I'm not," Eeyore said. "One mustn't complain."

"I'll save you!" Dramatically whipping off his overcoat, Christopher threw it to the ground, ran along the bank, then dove into the water. But to his surprise—and pain—he didn't dive down far: the water was only a few feet deep. Christopher stood up, dripping once again. "Oh, right," he said, starting to smile. "I'm grown now." The smile grew wider as he realized how ridiculous he must have looked. And how little he cared. He started to laugh—lightly at first; then the laugh grew and grew until tears spilled from the corners of his eyes. Standing there, wiping them away, Christopher tried to remember the last time he had laughed that hard. Sadly, he honestly had no idea.

"Laughing at my misfortune. Oh, well," Eeyore said.

Eeyore's ho-hum remark snapped Christopher back to the present, and he quickly waded over to the donkey. Grabbing him just before he went over the waterfall, Christopher then carried him back to the riverbank. Wringing him out like one might wring out a dishcloth, Christopher gently placed Eeyore on the ground.

"Hello, Eeyore," he said.

"Hello, Heffalump," Eeyore replied.

Christopher smiled, the feeling less foreign this time around. "I'm not a Heffalump," he said. "I'm Christopher Robin, the one who used to try and cheer you up."

Eeyore shrugged. "I don't remember being cheery."

Knowing it would do no good to try to explain, Christopher changed the subject. "How did you end up in the water?" he asked instead.

"Woke up. Windy. House blew down. Fell in the river. Can't swim." Eeyore listed his woes matter-of-factly, with no emotion. "Just another Windsday morning for me." In the distance, a Heffalump—or whatever it had been that Christopher had heard the night before—let out a terrible roar. Eeyore looked over at Christopher. "It's your fellow Heffalumps calling you home."

Rather than attempt to once again explain that he was *not* a Heffalump, Christopher decided to try instead to get to the bottom of this very puzzling mystery of the missing friends. Narrowing his eyes, he put a finger to his chin. When he was a boy, he and Pooh would play detective. Putting a finger to one's chin was always a good way to start. "So," he said, "everyone woke up. It was a Windsday." Eeyore nodded. "And where does everyone go on a Windsday?" Picking Eeyore up at that point, Christopher slung him over his shoulder and began to walk back toward Pooh Sticks Bridge.

From over Christopher's shoulder, Eeyore sighed. "Beats me," he said. "Nobody invites me anywhere."

Well, Christopher thought, *like it or not, Eeyore, you're coming with me now. We're going to find out where everyone goes on a Windsday.* And hopefully, wherever that place was, it would be where Christopher would find Pooh.

Chapter Ten

With a reluctant and rather morose Eeyore in tow, Christopher left the stream and headed back into the woods. He wasn't quite sure, but it *seemed* as though the fog had thinned a bit overnight, and he was beginning to recognize his surroundings more and more. It was as though the Hundred-Acre Wood were coming back to life.

Well, at least some of it appeared to be.

Pushing through a particularly prickly patch of bushes, Christopher stumbled into a clearing in the woods. He glanced around. The place looked vaguely familiar. Then his eyes fell on a pile of wood at the base of one of the taller trees.

"Owl's house," Christopher said, realizing exactly where they were. "It's fallen out of the tree."

Just then, the same awful noise Christopher and

Eeyore had heard by the river echoed through the woods. Only this time it sounded more awful and frightening—if that was possible.

"It must be digesting," Eeyore said.

"Heffalumps aren't real," Christopher said, looking down at the donkey. But even as he said those words, he knew they sounded flat. He was beginning to think that Heffalumps *were* real. Real and, as another whiney roar sounded, too close for his own comfort.

Trying to ignore the sound, Christopher began to creep toward Owl's house, which lay in disrepair. It was a mess. Wood had splintered everywhere, and the roof had come off in the fall. Calling out Owl's name, Christopher moved closer to it until he was almost beside it. Another Heffalump roar sent him tumbling back. Eeyore followed close behind. For a moment, neither moved.

Then, summoning his courage, Christopher crossed the clearing in a few long strides. He stopped right next to the house. Peering around, he saw a weather vane tilting off the side of the roof. It was bent, the metal twisted and contorted by the strong winds that had clearly sent Owl's house flying. As Christopher watched, another gust of wind blew through the clearing. The weather vane strained against the roof, the air rushing through the bent metal and causing it to scrape against the roof. The resulting sound was the roar of the "Heffalumps."

"It's just the weather vane!" Christopher cried out triumphantly when he realized what was happening. He *had* been right about Heffalumps! They didn't exist! The wind kicked up a notch and the resulting "Heffalump" roar had Eeyore folding his ears over his eyes and cringing. Quickly, Christopher climbed over the roof and reached out a hand, stopping the weather vane's movements.

Instantly, the horrible screeching noise stopped as well.

Eeyore peeked up from behind his long, floppy ears. "Huh," he said, sounding as impressed as Eeyore ever sounded. "Will you look at that." Slowly, he climbed up onto the roof to take a closer look.

"But no Owl," Christopher said as he pulled the weather vane free of the roof so that the dreaded noise would stop for good. Freed from the fear of a Heffalump attack, Christopher focused back on the reason he was in the Hundred-Acre Wood in the first place.

"What happened to everyone?" Christopher asked.

"If only Christopher Robin were here," Eeyore answered. "He would know."

"I *am* Christopher Robin," Christopher pointed out.

Eeyore raised an eyebrow. "You should be able to tell us then," he said, sounding rather unconvinced.

Taking the donkey's words as a challenge, Christopher walked around Owl's disheveled house, looking for signs. He peered through the hole in the roof. He took stock of the table and the chairs that now lay on their sides. Backing up, he tripped and nearly fell over an uneven plank on the side of the house. As he caught his balance, his eyes fell on a single shutter that had blown free and was lying on the ground, covered in mud—and what looked like footprints.

Suddenly, Christopher let out a triumphant shout. He knew what had happened. "They were all here," he said, telling Eeyore his theory. He pointed to the table through the hole and then at the plank. "Rabbit's carrots. And someone was bouncing. Tigger."

"Obvious," Eeyore said, unimpressed.

Christopher pointed at the shutter as he delivered his conclusion: "It must've broken free, flown up, and slammed into the weather vane. Everybody, of course, thought it was a Heffalump! Panicked, they flew out the door." As he spoke, he acted out his words, jumping at an unheard noise and then looking around, frightened. He pointed to the door and a small pile of haycorn shells. "Haycorn shells. A whole trail of them."

"Follow them and we'll find Piglet," Eeyore said before Christopher could get the words out.

Christopher stopped what he was doing and gave the donkey a disgruntled glare. "Now *that* was obvious," he muttered under his breath. Then, grabbing Eeyore, he put him under his arm and took off in pursuit of the haycorn trail. They were on the hunt!

* * *

As they moved through the woods, following the trail of haycorns left behind by Piglet, Christopher couldn't help smiling. It felt nice to be out doing something, rather than sitting behind a desk. He was being useful and productive. And, he thought—unable to completely let go of the professional man he had become—he was being rather efficient about it. In the sky above, the sun began to peek out from behind the clouds.

"Here's another one!" Christopher shouted, spotting a haycorn. "And another!" The haycorns were being uncovered faster and faster.

Suddenly, Christopher heard an unmistakable crunching sound. He cocked his head. It wasn't the sound of someone crunching just anything. It was the sound of someone crunching *haycorns*. He took a few steps forward. The noise appeared to be coming from behind a row of trees. Christopher moved closer; then he peeked around the trunk.

And sure enough, sitting there on a rock, eating haycorns at a rapid pace—with a very stressed expression on his little face—was Piglet.

Hearing the rustling caused by Christopher's footsteps, Piglet looked up, startled. "Who is it? Who's th-there?" he stammered.

Christopher set Eeyore down and nudged him toward the clearing. By the way the small pig was eating the haycorns, Christopher knew his old friend was already on edge. If Piglet saw a familiar face first, he might begin to calm down.

"It's just me," Eeyore said, slowly ambling forward.

Piglet's eyes lit up. "Eeyore!" he shouted in a squeaky voice. "Thank goodness it's you."

"Never has anybody cared so much," Eeyore replied in his typical sad way.

Watching from behind the tree, Christopher saw Piglet visibly relax. Taking that as a good sign, he stepped forward. But unfortunately, thanks to the now present sun, the first thing Piglet saw was a large shadow that seemed to tower monstrously over him. Just as Eeyore had done, Piglet mistook Christopher for a Heffalump and let out a high-pitched scream.

"Piglet," Christopher said as reassuringly as he could. He then took another step forward so he was no longer in the shadows. "It's just me. It's Christopher Robin."

His words did nothing to calm the tiny creature. "Don't—don't move," he squeaked. "And maybe it won't eat us."

Reaching into his pocket, Christopher dug out one of the many haycorns he had collected as they followed Piglet's trail. He held it out. "Here," he said. "Would a Heffalump offer you a haycorn?"

Piglet furrowed his brow thoughtfully. "It would . . . if it were trying to trick me!" Christopher let out a chuckle, thinking that Piglet had to be kidding. But then, quick as a wink, Piglet grabbed the haycorn and took off. Luckily for Christopher, the little pig couldn't get very far very fast. Christopher watched him run toward a hole at the top of a fallen tree, then scramble inside.

Following him over to the log, Christopher could hear muffled voices inside. He bent down so his head was closer to the opening. The voices became more distinct and he quickly made out Rabbit's. "Piglet," he was saying, "you have a head full of fluff! You've led it right to us. Now we're stuffed!"

Christopher leaned farther over. "Hello, everyone!" he said, speaking into the log.

In response, Tigger bounded out. His paws were up in a fighting stance, and he was bouncing more than usual so that he looked like a blur of orange and black. But while Tigger was pretending to be tough, especially when he spoke, it was clear he was terrified. His eyes were wide and his voice distinctly shaky: "I'll pounce ya, I'll pound ya—"

"Tigger," Christopher said, all too familiar now with going unrecognized, "it's me. Christopher Robin." Then he squatted down and stuck his head right into the opening of the hollow tree. Inside, huddled together, was the gang: Rabbit, Owl, Kanga, Roo, and, of course, Piglet. Upon seeing Christopher's disembodied head, they shrieked in unison.

But then, slowly, the shrieks grew quieter. Inside the log, they looked at one another. Then at Christopher. Then back to each other. Could it be? Could Christopher Robin have returned? Finally, Eeyore lumbered over. Stretching out his neck so that he was nose-to-nose with Christopher, he peered into his eyes.

"It is Christopher Robin," he said with a nod. "You can see it in his eyes now."

One by one, the rest of the group stepped up to take their own look at Christopher. He waited patiently. He let Tigger squeeze his nose and Roo touch his face. Satisfied, they stepped back so Owl could finally approach.

The wise old bird took his time. He leaned in close. Then he pulled back. Then he leaned in close again, his huge eyes unblinking. Finally, he nodded. "Ah, yes," he said. "I see it. Quite clear. Never really doubted it at all." Christopher opened his mouth to object but stopped himself. Owl went on. "Would you like to join us, Christopher Robin? We're hiding from the Heffalump."

"But the Heffalump was just your old weather vane, Owl!" Christopher said, straightening to his full height.

Popping his head out of a hole in the top of the log, Rabbit tsked. "Oh, dear," he said to the others. "He's addled in the brain. Happens to the elderly." He turned his attention to Christopher. Speaking to him as though he were a child, he explained that a weather vane and a Heffalump are two different things.

"Poor old thing," Kanga said in her kind, motherly way. She raised her voice, as though speaking to someone who was hard of hearing. "A Heffalump really isn't a weather vane, dear," she said.

Christopher stood there, not sure whether to laugh or cry. He knew he looked different. He knew he was significantly older than he had been the last time he had visited the Hundred-Acre Wood. But he wasn't an invalid. And he hadn't lost his hearing—or his mind. But before he could point any of this out, the rest of the group added their two cents' worth about the obvious differences between weather vanes and Heffalumps.

"That's right," Tigger agreed. "The beast is real. We heard it this morning; woke us all up. It's gotten loose again."

Owl nodded. "And worse, Pooh has gone missing."

Popping his head out of his mother's pouch, Roo glanced nervously around. "And I'm—I'm not leaving until it's gone for good," he said. His big eyes were full of fear.

"But there's no such thing as monsters," Christopher said when they had all spoken, trying to reassure them. It didn't work. Instead, they all shrank back, just as scared as ever. Telling them the monster wasn't real wasn't going to get him anywhere. He needed to take their collective fear seriously if he was going to get them to stop shaking and trust him. "Yes, right. No monsters. Except, of course, for Heffalumps."

"And Woozles," Owl added.

Christopher nodded. "Err, yes," he agreed. "And Woozles. And you're right, Roo. We've got a scary Heffalump here, and it's time I defeated it." He took a step back. Ignoring a look from Eeyore, who knew that the creature was, in fact, not real, he looked around the clearing for a "Heffalump." Spotting a tall oak tree just beyond the edge of the clearing, he pointed at it. "Ahh!" he shouted, trying his best to sound and look scared while confronting a tree. "There it is! Stop, Heffalump!" He knew he looked ridiculous. Even Eeyore was rolling his eyes. "You're either part of the problem or part of the solution," he hissed under his breath.

Eeyore shrugged. "Now which sounds like me?"

Christopher shot him another look. If he was going to defeat the Heffalump, he was going to have to be tricky about it. Grabbing his umbrella and his briefcase, he pretended to chase the Heffalump out of the clearing. Over his shoulder, he shouted a promise to put an end to the Heffalump once and for all. Then he disappeared into the trees.

CHAPTER ELEVEN

Christopher couldn't believe it had come to this. He was about to fight the Heffalump. Which, of course, was an impossibility, since there were no such things as Heffalumps. So what he was really fighting was his overcoat, stuffed with leaves and cinched with his belt.

"This is complete silliness," Christopher said as he pulled out his umbrella and began dragging the Heffalump back toward the edge of the clearing. He needed everyone to witness his fight as he defeated the scary creature, but he didn't want those watching to get so close that they would be able to see what he was actually fighting.

Throwing his briefcase on the ground, he stepped onto it and turned so his back was to the log and his audience across the clearing. Then he began to "fight" the Heffalump. Brandishing his umbrella like a sword, he swung wildly. "Hey you, Heffalump!" Christopher shouted. "I'll teach you to scare my friends!" Switching roles, Christopher roared back in response as if he were the Heffalump.

Back and forth Christopher went, first playing the part of the hero, then the part of the Heffalump. He stomped his foot and let out louder and louder roars. Then he would call out in fear as if he were being attacked. After a while, Christopher found himself enjoying the playacting. He forgot the others were watching. He forgot that the Heffalump wasn't real. He forgot about Winslow Luggage and the impending employee cuts and the fact that he was missing time with his family. He lost himself in just having fun.

"Oh, no!" he shouted, whacking desperately at the creature as though it were drawing closer. "I'm done for! Oh, no you don't!" He swung the umbrella harder and harder. Swooping down, he grabbed some leaves and threw them up into the air so it appeared as though he had wounded the creature.

Watching him from the safety of the log, the others waited to see what would happen. Tigger, never good at standing still even in a calm situation, was bouncing up and down frantically. "Oh, boy," he said excitedly. "He sure is giving that Heffalump a pounding! Oooh! I'd love to get in there and give that monster a wallop or two of my own!" He raised up his paws and brandished them like a boxer.

"Why don't you?" Kanga asked.

Tigger looked down, suddenly not quite as brave as he had been a moment before. "Um . . . well," he stammered. Then he pointed at Christopher, who, as they watched, launched himself off the ground where he had fallen. "Christopher's got it under control," Tigger observed.

Which, technically, was true—although Christopher was giving himself quite the beating. Landing next to Eeyore, he winced as his foot twisted slightly beneath him. Caught up in the fun of it, he had forgotten that he wasn't a seven-year-old boy playing make-believe. His bones and body weren't as forgiving.

"Pathetic," Eeyore said, catching the wince Christopher displayed but remaining unimpressed by the show. "That's what it is."

In response, Christopher pretended to be dragged backward by the Heffalump. His fingers clawed at the ground and then, accidentally, he grabbed Eeyore's tail. There was a tearing sound, and the donkey's tail came off in his hand.

"There goes the tail," Eeyore intoned. "Typical."

"Oh, no! Not the tail!" Christopher cried, using the mistake to up the action and build to the climax of the fight. At the log, the gang watched with wide eyes, nervous—and curious—to see what would happen next. While Eeyore found it pathetic, the others were buying the fight hook, line, and sinker. Not wanting to let down his audience, Christopher threw everything he had into the final moments of the fight. "Take that you stupid, self-centered, joyless beast! I'm not afraid of you! You rotten, stinking *Heffaluuuuuump!*" His voice trailed off as silence descended over the clearing.

A moment later, Christopher's overcoat flew up into

the air and then slowly floated down, down—all the way down to the ground.

"Did the Heffalump beat him, Mommy?" Roo asked when Christopher didn't immediately appear. His lower lip quivered and he began to sniffle.

All around him, the others looked just as sad. They had been able to see most of what was going on, but being on the log had kept them from seeing everything. From those last sounds, it seemed as though Christopher had tried valiantly to take on a Heffalump. But . . . had it been enough?

"Victory is ours!"

Christopher's triumphant voice startled everyone and they looked over to the edge of the woods. Dirty and disheveled, but with a huge smile on his face, Christopher burst into the center of the clearing.

"Hip-hip-hooray!" the others hollered back, while tumbling out of the log. "Hip-hip-hooray!"

"T-t-time for a celebration?" Piglet asked.

Christopher smiled. "Great idea!" he said, pleased to have made everyone happy. He had never realized how satisfying defeating a fake monster could be. But then his smile faded, and he frowned. "But I still have to find Pooh."

"You're Christopher Robin," Roo said, all traces of his earlier worries subsiding. "You'll find him Somewhere."

Staring down at the young kangaroo, Christopher wished he had as much faith in himself as the others now did. But he had already been all over the woods. It seemed unlikely he would find Pooh easily. But then Roo's words sank in. Suddenly, Christopher's face brightened. "That's it, Roo!" he cried. "He's waiting for Somewhere to come to him!"

* * *

Christopher stopped and stared at the grassy hill ahead of him. Beside him, the rest of the group looked on, watching to see what he would do next. They had helped him get back to the Enchanted Place—the place he had said good-bye to Pooh all those years ago—but somehow, they sensed that he had to take the final few steps on his own.

Christopher put down his dirty overcoat and briefcase, then nodded to the others. After that he began to walk up the small hill. He was surprised to find that he was oddly nervous, as though he were walking up the hill to meet a stranger, not a childhood friend. But then he realized that it wasn't nerves. It was guilt. The only reason Pooh had come out here was because Christopher had sent him away.

Upon cresting the top of the hill, Christopher smiled. There, just as he had imagined he would be, was Pooh. The bear was sitting on their log, his back to Christopher. In his hand, he held the red balloon.

"Hello, Pooh," Christopher said softly as he came up behind the bear.

Pooh turned and smiled at him, as though he had been waiting. "Hello, Christopher Robin," he replied.

For a long moment, the pair of friends just looked at each other. Then, hesitantly, Christopher stepped forward. His voice was soft and full of remorse when he spoke. "I'm sorry, Pooh. I'm so terribly sorry. I never should have yelled at you."

"But I am a Bear of a Very Little Brain," Pooh replied. His answer wasn't spoken in an accusatory or angry manner. It was in a matter-of-fact tone, one of understanding, which made Christopher's heart ache even more.

He shook his head. "You are," he said, "I think, a Bear of Very Big Heart." Touched by Christopher's words, Pooh lowered his head, a flush rising on his chubby cheeks. Taking that as a sign he had been forgiven, Christopher moved around the log. "You'll be glad to know everyone's safe and sound. They were hiding from a Heffalump, which turned out to be, well, me. And Owl's weather vane." He sat down beside Pooh. Together they stared out at the horizon. The fog was gone, replaced by bright sunshine that shone down over the wood, making it glow. "Thank you for waiting for me."

"It's always a sunny day when Christopher Robin comes out to play," Pooh said, giving his friend a big smile.

Christopher tried to smile back, but he still felt bad. "I'm not so sure of that," he finally said, staring down at his hands. Beneath the dirt, blisters were forming from his "fight" with the Heffalump. "I'm not who I used to be."

Pooh shook his head. "But of course you are," he said. "You're our friend. Why, look at how you saved everyone today. You're our hero."

Raising his eyes, Christopher met Pooh's gaze. The bear was looking at him with absolute trust and faith. It was the way Evelyn used to look at him. The way Madeline *still* looked at him from time to time. It was the way his team looked at him. But for so long, he hadn't noticed. Worse still, he hadn't truly cared. Hearing his childhood friend call him a hero felt simultaneously wonderful and like the greatest lie ever told. "I'm not a hero, Pooh," he finally said, his voice barely a whisper. "I'm . . . lost."

Pooh's response was quick and perfect. "I found you, didn't I?" he said. Leaning over, he wrapped his arms around Christopher as far as they could go. Then he squeezed.

In the bear's embrace, Christopher felt his body

stiffen. He shifted awkwardly, unsure what to do. And then, once more, he thought of Evelyn. Of the first hug they had shared when they began dating. How he had melted into it and how it had felt like home. He thought of the first time he held Madeline in his arms. She had been so small—and he had been so scared that he would break her. But she, too, had just melted into him. His heart had never been fuller than in that moment.

And suddenly, just like that, something inside Christopher shifted. His heart, closed for so long, opened. Leaning down so he could get a better angle, he squeezed Pooh right back. The bear gave a long, happy sigh, and Christopher felt him melt against his side. Turning them both so they could face the valley below, Christopher watched as the sun began to sink beneath the horizon. His shoulders, no longer weighed down by incredible worry, felt light. His heart, open to possibility, felt strong and young once more. As the sun slipped farther and farther away (and the stars came out), Christopher allowed himself to relax—and just before his eyes shut and he drifted off to sleep, with

Pooh still beside him, Christopher realized . . . he was, for the moment, happy.

* * *

Unfortunately, the feeling was short-lived. It lasted for only a night.

Waking with a start, Christopher saw that sun was up. Beside him, Pooh was still sleeping. Sitting bolt upright, Christopher startled Piglet, who had been sent by the others to wake the two friends. The skittish pig leaped backward as Christopher's eyes grew wide and he jumped to his feet.

"Oh, no. Oh, no. Oh, no!" he cried. His shoulders instantly tensed and his heart began to race at its normal anxious speed. He had spent the night in the Hundred-Acre Wood! That wasn't good. That wasn't good at all. He needed to be in London!

"What is it?" Pooh asked, slowly waking up.

"It's tomorrow!" Christopher replied.

Pooh looked confused. "It's usually Today," he pointed out.

Despite the current waves of panic washing over him, Christopher couldn't help smiling at the bear's rationale. "Well, yes," he agreed. "Of course, it's today. Which means I slept over, and I need to be at the office in—" He looked down at his watch. It was broken. Letting out a yelp, he ran a hand through his already disheveled hair. "How could I have let this happen? And my things!"

As he began to race helplessly around the log, Owl, Rabbit, Eeyore, and the others walked up. They had also spent the night nearby. Having found Christopher Robin again, they didn't want to lose him. But as they approached, it was clear that he was going to be leaving again soon.

"Don't you worry," Owl said. "As my old uncle Orville used to say, 'Worry is the way to concern.' " His head twisted to the side and he blinked his big eyes. "Or was it, 'Concern is the way to confusion'? Or, no, it was—"

Pushing past Owl, the rest of the gang walked up to Christopher. They had his overcoat and briefcase.

Kanga nodded toward them and smiled in her sweet, kind way. "We got all your belongings nice and dry now," she said.

Christopher smiled back, touched by their thoughtfulness. "Thank you," he said, taking the briefcase. Instantly, his expression changed. Once again, Christopher looked like a serious businessman, not a happy-go-lucky boy playing make-believe in the woods. "I couldn't forget my case of Important Things. I'm sorry I have to go. But I've already stayed far too long." Putting on his overcoat, he stuffed a hand into his pocket. His fingers closed around a round metal object. His compass. Pulling it out, he held it out to Pooh. "You keep this. So, if anyone goes missing again, you can find them."

"Thank you, Christopher Robin," Pooh said. Then, very seriously, as though he were presenting something of great value, Pooh turned and grabbed the red balloon from where he had tied it to the log. "And you should take this. For Madeline."

Instinctively, Christopher started to shake his

head no. But looking at his old friend, he stopped and, instead, reached out and took the balloon.

"What's a Madeline?" Roo asked. He had been hoping that he would maybe get to play with the red balloon and was slightly disappointed it was going away with Christopher Robin. "Is she more important than your case of Important Things?"

"Well, yes, of course. Absolutely," Christopher replied. "She means the world to me."

"Then why isn't she with you?" Roo asked.

Before Christopher could answer, Pooh stepped forward. He put a paw on Roo's shoulder. "She has work to do, Roo," he said in his very serious Pooh voice, repeating what Christopher had said to him back at the country house. Hearing it from Pooh, Christopher realized how terrible it sounded.

Kanga seemed to agree. "Oh, the poor dear," she said sadly.

"No, she—" Christopher stammered, trying to make it sound better but knowing he couldn't. "She . . . likes work." He stopped and sighed. He was wasting time.

"Look, I've got to rush. Good-bye everyone. Nice to see you again." And then, before he could change his mind or start to feel bad at abandoning his newly found friends, Christopher turned and walked away.

Behind him, the animals watched him go with wide eyes. Silence descended on the hill. Reaching up, Piglet took Pooh's paw in his own. It looked like they were going to have to find a way to do without Christopher Robin—again.

Chapter Twelve

Christopher quickly made his way back to the tree and the green door that would bring him home. Bending down, he cringed as pain shot through his joints. His attack on the Heffalump had been intense and his body, now older and less resilient, was letting him know that he had pushed it. Biting back a groan, he made his way through the door, emerging a moment later in the woods behind his family's country home. Out of habit, he looked down at his watch. It was still broken. But it didn't matter. He knew that if he were going to make the train and get back to the city, he had to rush.

Picking up his pace, he hurried through the woods. The red balloon bobbed and weaved in the air behind him. Catching a flash of red, Christopher felt a fresh wave of guilt as he realized how quickly he had left

Pooh and the others. A part of him longed to have stayed, enjoying the freedom he had felt for that brief time. But stepping out of the woods and onto the lawn, he caught sight of the house. It was a visible reminder of his real-life responsibilities.

Christopher held his breath as he crossed the lawn. The last thing he needed was to attract the attention of Evelyn or Madeline. They would have so many questions. But just as he reached the house, he caught sight of his old bike leaning against the siding. The balloon string pulled at his wrist. Glancing around to make sure he was still in the clear, he walked over and quickly tied the balloon to the handlebars of the bike. It would be a nice surprise for Madeline when she came outside.

"Father!"

Madeline's high-pitched shriek of happiness stopped Christopher just as he turned to go. Looking up, he saw his daughter's face peering down at him from her bedroom window. Foolishly, as though he would somehow become instantly invisible, Christopher ducked down. But Madeline could still see him.

"Father?" she repeated, opening the window and peering down. "What are you doing here?"

Christopher looked up at Madeline and then back toward the road. He could make a run for it. Pretend he didn't see her or hear her. He groaned. That was the stupidest thought he had ever had. Of course he couldn't just run away from his daughter.

"Were you in the woods?" Madeline called down.

"Yes, but . . ." Christopher stammered, not sure what to say. It wasn't like he could just come out and explain that he went through a door to another part of the woods and had been playing with his childhood animal friends for the past day. That sounded crazy!

Just then, Evelyn stepped outside. Seeing her husband, she cocked her head in confusion—and a flicker of hope flashed in her eyes. It dimmed as Christopher shrugged apologetically. "I'm terribly sorry," he said to both his wife and daughter, "but I have to go."

"You can't stay?" Madeline's voice had grown smaller and she was looking down at him now with sadness, not hope.

The expression broke Christopher's heart and he silently cursed himself for stopping to tie that balloon. If he had just kept going, he wouldn't be standing there now, trying to explain himself to his family. "No, darling," he said finally. "I have an eleven o'clock meeting I'm terribly late for."

Madeline's face crumpled. Pushing back, she slid the window shut and disappeared from view. Beside him, he heard Evelyn sigh deeply. "Sorry," he apologized again. "I didn't mean for her to see me. But I need to be on the next train." Even as the words left his mouth, he knew his excuse sounded weak. To his family, it seemed as if he had come out suddenly, only to turn around and leave.

Evelyn stared back at him for a long, silent moment. Her eyes were cold, and when she finally spoke, her voice was icy. "Well, then you better go," she said.

"There's a good explanation for this," Christopher said. "I promise."

"I'd love to hear it," Evelyn said, folding her arms, waiting.

Christopher looked back at her, trying to see if there was any pity behind the coldness in Evelyn's eyes. He did want to tell her. He wanted to tell her everything. He wanted to apologize, and he wanted her to understand that he wasn't trying to mess up. He wanted to tell her about his adventures in the Hundred-Acre Wood and how he had defeated the Heffalump and found Winnie the Pooh. When they had first started dating and when they had first been married, he *would* have told her. He would have told her and known that she would have believed him and been enchanted. But as he continued to look in her eyes, he realized that he had pushed her too far away. That she was lost to him in a way that he couldn't quite grasp. And while he knew it was entirely his fault, the pain was still terrible. "I can't," he said softly.

The silence that followed was deafening.

Turning to go inside, Evelyn looked back over her shoulder. There was nothing left in her eyes but disappointment. It was worse than the look she had been giving him. "I was thinking that Madeline and I should stay here longer," she said. "The country's good for her. For us."

Christopher felt the blood drain from his face. He thought back to the night in the house when he had stood with the suitcases, worrying that he had pushed too far. Maybe he hadn't then, but it certainly seemed like he had now. And he couldn't really blame Evelyn.

"Do you really think that's best?" Christopher wondered.

"I do."

"For how long?" he asked, not actually wanting to hear the answer.

Evelyn shrugged. "I don't know, Christopher." Then she walked up the steps and opened the back door. Looking down at her watch, she sighed. "You're going to miss your train." Then, without another word, she entered the house, letting the door slam shut behind her.

For one long moment, Christopher stayed there, rooted to the spot. His breath hitched in his chest and he felt as though he were drowning in quicksand. He had to go. He had to. It was the responsible thing to do.

If he didn't make the meeting, he would be fired and the company would probably shut its doors. But if he *did* go, what was going to happen to his marriage? To his life?

Taking one last look up at the window of his daughter's bedroom, Christopher let out a sad sigh. Then he turned and ran down the drive. As his feet pounded the ground, he couldn't help wondering: had he just ruined everything?

* * *

Madeline stared at the bookshelf in front of her. In her hand, she held one of her assigned summer-reading textbooks. She had read it cover to cover and written the required report. In fact, she had read every one of her summer-reading books and done all the reports. It was time to put the books away. But for some reason, she found herself hesitating.

She still couldn't believe her father had been there—in the country. And that he had just left. She didn't understand. Had she done something wrong? Had she said something wrong? She had diligently done all her work because that was what Father had wanted. She had only gone on one bike ride so far. Why hadn't he stayed? She looked at the book in her hand. She liked books because books had answers. They made sense. Her father didn't make sense to her—not anymore, at least.

The sound of the stairs creaking startled Madeline, and she looked over her shoulder to see her mother walking up them with a glass of milk and a plate of cookies. Crossing the landing, she held out the treats.

"I believe I am done with these for now," Madeline said, not taking one of the offered treats.

"Good! You know these books like the back of your hand," Evelyn said, trying to sound cheerful. The look on her daughter's face was heartbreaking. She was a little girl. She was a little girl spending time in the country. But instead of being outside in the fresh air, she was inside, studying. As Evelyn watched, Madeline carefully shelved the final book and then stepped back. "Darling," Evelyn asked, "what would you *like* to do?"

Madeline cocked her head. What would she *like* to do? She honestly didn't know. Now that she was done with her work, she didn't have anything she *had* to do. She sighed. What she really wanted to do was see her father. But he had gone back to the city, so that wasn't a possibility. She looked around the room, her eyes landing on a box of toys.

"I'd like to play," she said with a determined nod.

"You would?" Evelyn said, surprised. Hope flooded through her. Perhaps Christopher's brief drop-in hadn't devastated Madeline as much as she thought it had. Maybe she could allow herself to be a child for once and relax. But then Madeline went on and the hope for such a result faded.

"Yes," Madeline answered, as though she were responding to a test question. "I shall play better and harder than any child has ever played."

"It can also be fun?" Evelyn said.

Madeline shrugged. "Agreed. It shall also be fun."

Evelyn sighed. There was so much of Christopher in

Madeline. When she had been a baby, Evelyn thought that was sweet and would stare at her daughter's face for hours, laughing at the similar expressions that would flit across both her husband's and her daughter's faces. But now, she realized, it was no longer a good thing. If Evelyn didn't do something, her daughter was going to grow up too fast. "Go out and play," she said, trying to keep the sadness out of her voice. "We'll have tea later."

Pleased to have directions to follow, Madeline turned and marched outside. Watching her go, Evelyn silently cursed Christopher. *You should be here to fix this*, she thought. *You should be here to play with your daughter.* But instead, he had chosen work—again.

* * *

Pooh felt funny. He couldn't quite put a paw on it, but ever since Christopher had left the Hundred-Acre Wood, Pooh had felt strange. Walking back to Piglet's house, he thought maybe he was just hungry. After all, he hadn't had honey in quite some time, and a bear needed honey to feel like himself.

Reaching into Piglet's cupboards, he felt around for a lone jar of the sweet nectar. But his search came up empty. Turning to his friend, Pooh let out a very un-Pooh-like sigh. "I don't feel very much like Pooh today."

Piglet walked over and gently took Pooh's paw in his. "There, there," he said softly. "I'll bring you tea and honey until you do."

Pooh nodded. Tea and honey *did* sound nice. Maybe if he had enough of both, the funny feeling in his stomach would go away. He wished, though, that Christopher could have stayed and had some tea and honey with him. It had been nice to have his friend back. Pooh hadn't realized how strange the Hundred-Acre Wood had been without him around. But now that he was gone, the absence was pronounced. Already, fog had begun to roll back in through the trees and the sun seemed less bright.

Hearing a commotion outside, Pooh turned just in time to see Tigger bounce into Piglet's house, holding a large pot of honey. He had a huge smile on his face and was bounding around even more than usual.

Apparently, the funny feeling Pooh had was not felt by all. "Hello, friends!" Tigger said.

"Just in time!" Pooh said, grabbing the pot and lifting it to his face. But instead of getting a mouthful of honey, he got bonked in the nose by something. Pulling his head back, he saw that it was the big brown folder Christopher Robin had been carrying around with him. "Tigger! Why did you take these out of the case of Important Things?" Pooh asked.

Tigger shrugged. "Just taking up space!" he answered. "Needed to get rid of this flippity-flap paper. Make room for the real Important Stuff."

"What will happen to Christopher Robin without them?" Piglet asked. His voice squeaked nervously and he began to search for haycorns.

Pooh put a paw to his Thinking Spot. This wasn't good. He couldn't remember exactly what Christopher had said—probably due to the lack of honey clouding his thoughts—but he knew that Christopher needed those papers. He tapped his Thinking Spot harder and harder. *Think, think, think*, he said to himself. What was going to happen to Christopher Robin? And then he let out a shout. He remembered! "Christopher said that a Woozle was going to eat him for breakfast!"

The others gasped.

Grabbing the brown folder, Pooh walked toward the door. He had to get this stuff back to Christopher before he got eaten! Turning to the others, he signaled for them to follow. They needed to find Christopher—before it was too late!

* * *

Madeline had decided she was going to play tennis. In this case, she had replaced a tennis ball with the red balloon she had found tied to her bike. Tying it to the net on the tennis court behind the house, she whacked at the balloon with an old wooden racket she had found. Not good at doing anything merely halfway, she was pretending to not just play tennis, but rather play tennis at Wimbledon.

Lifting her arm up, she took on the role of announcer: "Madeline Robin, serving for the Wimbledon title," she called to her imaginary crowd. She brought down her arm, hitting the balloon down onto the court. "And it's an ace! She's won! The crowd goes wild!"

To her surprise, real cheering erupted from a bush along the court's edge. She cocked her head to listen. Then, tiptoeing closer, she tried to see inside the bush. But it was overgrown and she couldn't see anything through the thick greenery. "Hello?" she called out. No one answered. Growing more curious, Madeline picked up a ball and threw it into the bush.

A moment later, the ball came flying back.

"Who's in there?!" asked Madeline in a high-pitched voice. She knew she should never have agreed to go play. It was safer in the house. No invisible things threw balls at her or cheered when she pretended to hit a winning shot playing tennis.

Suddenly, the leaves on the bush began to rustle. Then Madeline heard voices. It sounded a lot like, "Stop pushing," and "Ouch." Then, before she could turn and run to find her mother, three creatures fell out of the bush and onto the court. Madeline shook her head, unsure if she were seeing things. But even after she blinked and pinched herself several times, the creatures—a small pig, a striped tiger of sorts, and a bear—were still standing there. They looked very much like she would imagine stuffed animals would look if they were real—which they couldn't be. . . .

"Hello," said the piglet.

"You must be Madeline," the bear said happily.

In turn, Madeline did the only thing she thought reasonable in such a situation: she screamed. Stumbling backward, Madeline tripped over something. Turning, she saw that the something she had tripped over was a small blue donkey.

"Sorry about that," the donkey said.

Once more, Madeline screamed. Only this time, the donkey startled. Then he began to run around in a circle. He would have kept going had he not hit the net and fallen in a heap on the court.

Holding up his paws, the bear came closer. "We're sorry," he said. "We didn't mean to interrupt your game."

Madeline took several deep breaths, trying to calm

herself. But she found it wasn't working. Because this didn't make sense. And she liked things that made sense. "You're . . . you're talking," she finally said.

"Me?" the bear asked, putting a paw to his chest. Then he shook his head. "No. I'm not talking. Well, I am now, I guess."

Madeline stared at the talking bear, her mind racing. While the situation was strange, there was something oddly familiar about the bear. It was like she had seen him somewhere before. She racked her brain. She didn't have any stuffed bears at home, so it couldn't be that. And she didn't have many friends—and the friends she did have mostly had dolls. But then, suddenly, she realized exactly why the bear looked familiar. "Wait!" she cried. "You're the bear in my father's drawings."

The bear smiled and nodded. "Winnie the Pooh," he said, introducing himself. "Pooh for short." He pointed at the others. "This is Piglet, Eeyore—"

"And I'm Tigger," the orange-and-black–striped creature said, jumping in and interrupting Pooh. "T-I-double G-UHR."

Madeline couldn't help smiling at the energetic creature. "What's a Tigger?" she asked.

The others let out a round of groans as Tigger began to bounce faster and faster around the court. A huge smile spread across his face and he burst into song. "*The wonderful thing about Tiggers,*" he sang, "*is Tiggers are wonderful things! Their tops are made out of rubber, their bottoms are made out of springs. They're bouncy, trouncy, flouncy, pouncy, fun, fun, fun, fun, fun. But the most wonderful thing about Tiggers is I'm the only one!*"

Madeline began clapping, laughing as Tigger finished his song with a flourish.

Beside her, Eeyore rolled his eyes. "He does that a lot."

"Well . . . hello," Madeline said, turning and smiling at everyone. While it was completely unexplainable, somehow her father's childhood drawings were here—and alive. And if Tigger's song was any indication, they seemed like they were quite a lot of fun.

"Did the red balloon make you happy?" Pooh asked,

taking the hello as a sign of instant friendship. "Balloons make me very happy."

"That was from you?" Madeline asked. She glanced over at the red balloon that was now, thanks to a round at Wimbledon, a bit deflated.

Pooh shook his head. "No, it was from Christopher Robin."

"My father was with you?" Madeline didn't bother to hide her surprise. Although, it *would* explain why her father had been slinking out of the woods so early in the morning. . . .

"Yes," Pooh answered. "He was helping me find my friends."

"*And* he saved us from the Heffalump," Piglet added.

Tigger bounced over. "But he left his Important Papers. Which *might* have been a smidge my fault."

"It *was* your fault," Eeyore replied.

In reaction to his deadpan response, Madeline tried to stifle a smile. She could tell already that Eeyore was the grump of the group. But a lovable one. The others were lovable, too. Her father's pictures flashed through her mind while she looked at them as they all explained the situation at hand. He had painted these animals in such a clear way but hadn't been able to capture them completely. Now that they were there and in front of her, Madeline was thrilled.

"So, we're going on an expotition to Lon Don," Piglet went on, mispronouncing the city.

Pooh nodded seriously. "If we don't get them to him, a Woozle at work is going to eat him for breakfast."

Madeline crinkled her nose. "A . . . Woo—?" Then she realized what, or rather who, Pooh was talking about. "You must mean Winslow." As the others continued to talk about their "expotition," Madeline half-listened, for she had become distracted. She was beginning to get an idea. If the others were going to London, she was going to go with them.

"Christopher Robin said we should go north."

Turning back, Madeline saw that the others had started to head toward the gate. She ran to catch up. "London is northwest, actually," she said, joining them. "But the train station is south."

Pooh looked down at the compass Christopher had given him. The arrow was pointing toward the *N*. He frowned. "South? I don't know south."

Madeline smiled. "Don't worry," she said, grabbing her bike that was resting along the wall of the house. "I do." Then, one by one, she plopped the animals into the basket on the bike's front handlebars. They were going on an "expotition."

But before they left, Madeline made sure to leave a note. After all, she *was* responsible. Racing into the house, she grabbed a piece of paper and quickly jotted down the following: *On an expotition to Father's work—got his papers. Be back soon.* Satisfied that that would make her mother happy, Madeline taped it to the back door and then raced outside.

Now they could *really* start the expedition.

CHAPTER THIRTEEN

Madeline was beginning to think that this "expotition" was going to be harder than she had thought. They had made it through town and to the train station without much trouble, but once they arrived at the station, things got a bit more complicated. Madeline knew she couldn't just walk up to the window with four talking animals. Luckily, Pooh knew what to do after his earlier train adventure with Christopher.

"Now we play nap time," Pooh said, quickly explaining how the game was played.

As the animals went floppy in her arms, Madeline approached the ticket counter. "One ticket please," she requested. "And a map of London." Reaching into her pocket for money to pay, Madeline accidentally dropped Eeyore. He landed on the ground with a thud.

"Ow," he mumbled. "Figures."

Plastering a smile on her face, Madeline quickly shoved the money at the attendant. Then, grabbing the ticket and the map, she darted off. They needed to get on the train before anything else like that happened.

Luckily, they made it onto the train and found an empty compartment. Settling in, Madeline quickly ordered five cups of tea—much to the porter's confusion—and then sat back as the train began to roll out of the station and into the surrounding countryside. Beside her, Pooh sat happily eating some honey while the others took in the landscape—except for Piglet, who was feeling a bit sick due to the rocking motion of the train.

As the train chugged toward the city, a light rain began to fall. It fell against the windows, making a nice rhythmic patter. A grey sky made the warmly lit compartment feel even more inviting and cozy. If it hadn't been for poor Piglet not feeling well, it would have been a perfectly lovely expedition.

"Don't think about it, Piglet," Tigger said as the

little pig tried not to throw up. "I know! I'll have that raindrop—" he added, pointing to a big droplet of water on the outside of the window. "And you have this one. Race ya to the bottom."

"It's worth a t-t-try," Piglet stammered, focusing on the window.

As the two friends began cheering on the raindrops, Madeline watched them, smiling. Then her smile faded. "There's going to be no fun like this at boarding school, Pooh," she said softly. For a short while she had been able to forget about the real world that awaited her once they left the country house. But now, as the city's skyline appeared on the horizon and she saw what fun her new friends were having, she couldn't help feeling a wave of sadness.

"Well, why not just not go?" Pooh said, as though that were obvious.

Madeline looked thoughtful. "If I can get these papers to Father," she said, her voice growing excited, "maybe he'll be so happy he won't make me go. Dreams don't come for free, Pooh, you've got to fight for them."

She paused, her father's words coming back to her. "Nothing comes from nothing."

Pooh nodded. "Oh, yes," he agreed, misinterpreting Madeline. "Nothing *always* leads to the very best Something."

"What?" Madeline said, the idea sounding foreign to her. Doing nothing was not an option in her house. "Who told you that?"

Pooh's answer surprised her. "Christopher Robin," he said.

Madeline shook her head. "That doesn't sound like Father," she said.

"That's because it's me, Pooh, speaking," Pooh replied, his tone innocent. Madeline began to smile despite herself. But then the bear went on: "He also said he's only happy if you're happy."

Madeline's smile faded completely. Now that was something that *definitely* did not sound like her father. "I think you are mistaken, Pooh," she said, trying not to cry.

But Pooh shook his head. "Oh, we heard him say it,

all right. Or my name's not Winnie the Pooh. Which it is. So, there you are."

Just then, Piglet let out a shout as his raindrop slid down the window first. Madeline looked over, happy for the distraction. She wanted to believe Pooh. But if her father cared so much about her, why was he always working instead of playing with her? And why, if he cared, would he want to send her away to boarding school? She turned and looked at the city looming in the distance. She didn't know the answers. At least not yet. But maybe, just maybe, if she helped him save his job—and those of his cohorts—she might just get him to change his mind.

* * *

Unfortunately, before Madeline could even think about changing her father's mind, she had to get from the train station to Winslow Luggage. Which meant she had to get a cab and somehow get the four animals to the building without being seen.

Getting the cab turned out to be easy enough. Madeline had seen her parents do it enough times before to know how to hail a big black car and then give the address of a destination. What turned out to be nearly impossible, however, was making sure that the four animals by her side didn't blow their cover. Besides Pooh, none of the animals had been to London before, and they wanted to watch and see everything as it passed by the taxi's windows.

Popping up, Tigger looked out the window. But instead of seeing the buildings outside, he caught sight of his reflection. Thinking he was seeing another Tigger, he stared, openmouthed. "Hey! What the–?"

"Tigger," Piglet hissed nervously. He looked over at the taxi driver just as the man's eyes returned to the road in front of him. He had definitely been looking at the back seat through the rearview mirror. "What are you doing?"

"I just saw the most preposterous imposter!" Tigger said.

Hearing voices, the cabbie glanced back over his shoulder. "What's that, love?" he asked.

Madeline gulped. "Oh, nothing," she said, trying to

sound completely normal and not at all like a young girl traveling alone in a taxi with four talking animals. "Just talking to myself." Then she leaned down and whispered in Tigger's ear. "Tigger, be quiet!"

But Tigger was not good at being quiet even in a normal situation. When presented with a possible imposter? Well, it was downright impossible. Even before Madeline could sit back, he was bouncing on his tail again. This time, he caught his image in the side-view mirror of the taxi. "There's another one! Look at him! His eyes are too close together!"

"Tigger!" Madeline whispered as loudly as she dared.

But the animal didn't even pretend to listen. He was far too focused on the "other Tigger" and the creature's flaws. "Look at that silly stripy hat and his little cauliflower ears." Tigger was growing more and more agitated. His paws were up in front of his nose and he was bouncing from the floor to the seat and back again as he tried to determine where the other Tigger was. Every time he bounced, the whole taxi shook.

Turning to see what the commotion was—and how one little girl could be making his taxi shake—the cab-driver caught sight of Tigger. He did a double take. But just as he looked back, Tigger ducked down again. The cabbie shook his head. He needed to lay off the caffeine and get some sleep. He was beginning to see things.

"I'm going to teach this copycat a lesson!" Tigger hissed from the floor of the taxi.

Piglet gulped. He had seen that look in Tigger's eyes before. Nothing good came from that look.

Just then, Tigger leaped up at the window. But as he jumped, he also let out a roar. This time, when the cab-bie turned around, there was no denying that he was not seeing things. There was, in fact, an orange-and-black-striped creature leaping and jumping around the back of his taxi. So the cabbie did what any person in his situation would do: he screamed.

And swerved—right into oncoming traffic.

Letting out another scream, he quickly wrenched the steering wheel back, narrowly missing a head-on collision with another taxi. In the back seat, Madeline and the animals went flying back and forth as the taxi continued its wild ride down the street.

"I'm never leaving the wood again!" Piglet cried, trying to clutch his now very upset stomach while somehow holding on to the door handle. Tigger, meanwhile, was still trying to fight his "imposter," and Pooh was being tossed helter-skelter all over the place. As the taxi made a particularly sharp swerve, Pooh went flying and ended up wedged in the small window of the taxi's partition.

"Hello," Pooh said jovially, when the cabbie caught sight of him out of the corner of his eye.

That was it. The last straw. The cabbie could only handle so much. Letting out another scream, he threw his hands in the air. Freed from any control, the steering wheel pulled to the left, and before anyone could do anything to stop it, the vehicle jumped the curb and went slamming into a newspaper stand.

As the engine coughed and then died, Madeline and the others crawled out of the back of the taxi. Brushing down her skirt, Madeline quickly checked the others to make sure they were all right. Behind her, a police officer raced up to the scene.

"You need to arrest this lot!" the cabbie shouted when the officer asked what was going on.

The policeman looked over at Madeline. She was standing still, an innocent expression on her face, with four stuffed animals in her arms. He looked back at the cabbie. "The little girl and her stuffed toys give you a fright, did they?" He didn't even bother to hide his amusement.

"Something's going on with that one," the cabbie said, shaking his head. "Something . . . spooky."

As the officer continued to question the cabbie, Madeline slowly began to back away from the accident. She was having a hard time keeping Tigger still and needed to get away. But how? Just then, she felt a tiny tug on her sleeve. Looking down, she saw that Piglet was pointing at something ahead of them.

"Madeline," he whispered. "Look! Doesn't that say '*Woozle*'?"

Looking to where Piglet was pointing, Madeline's eyes brightened. There, parked next to the curb half a block up, was a truck. On its side was written WINSLOW LUGGAGE. As she watched, a few deliverymen loaded some unfinished trunks into the back of the truck. She had an idea. But she had to act fast!

"Officer!" she said, getting the policeman's attention. "That's my father there!" She spun and pointed at what she thought was the first respectable-looking man she saw.

"All right then," the officer said, taking her at her word. "Off you pop. But be careful!"

Madeline flashed her most innocent and sweet smile. "I will! Thank you, officer!" Then, before the officer could rethink just sending her off, Madeline dashed down the street and slipped into the back of the truck moments before the deliverymen slammed the door shut.

Instantly, Madeline and the animals were plunged into darkness. But it didn't matter. If Madeline was right, which she usually was, this truck was heading toward the Winslow Luggage building. And her father.

Snuggling into an open trunk, Madeline made herself comfortable. Beside her, Pooh pulled out a small travel-sized jar of honey and began to eat. "This truck should take us right to Winslow's," Madeline explained as the truck rumbled along.

"You mean the Woozle?" Pooh asked through a mouthful of honey.

Madeline nodded. "That's right." Then she peered over the edge of her luggage trunk. The others were crammed together in a trunk down a ways. "How are you getting on in there?"

In response, there was a flurry of limbs and noses moving about—and then she saw Tigger's tail. "It's close quarters," Piglet called back as he swatted Tigger's tail out of the way. Then he pulled himself up so he could just barely see Madeline and Pooh. "But we're all right."

"Sit tight and we'll be there soon," Madeline called back.

Nodding, Piglet sank back down. He looked at the other two. They were crammed against the trunk's side, the big brown folder between them.

"What did she say?" Tigger asked Piglet.

"She said keep your tail out of my face," Piglet answered.

Eeyore cocked his head and narrowed his eyes. Beside him, Tigger did the same. "That doesn't sound like Madeline," he said, curious. "Let me ask her." He shifted in the trunk, preparing to launch himself up and out. Or at least up.

Piglet tugged on his leg and shook his head. He didn't want a repeat of the disastrous taxi ride. His stomach couldn't handle it. Sometimes he wished Tigger would just sit still. "We have to be quiet. Otherwise we'll get found out."

"Got it," Tigger said, nodding and crossing his heart. He popped up. "MADELINE!" he shouted, causing Piglet to cringe.

Just then, the truck ran over a pothole. The trunk

went bouncing up, connected to the vehicle by only a thin cord. Tigger went flying backward so far that his head ended up on the bottom of the trunk, wedged between Piglet and Eeyore, and his tail was flopping in the open. As the truck slammed down, so did the top of the trunk. It landed with a loud thud, right on Tigger's tail.

"ARRGGHHHH!" Tigger cried. And then he let out another cry as Piglet and Eeyore tried to pull his tail free. But it was no use. The truck was bouncing around too much. They couldn't get a grip. And then, just when they thought things couldn't get worse, the truck hit another huge pothole and sent the trunk bouncing down the length of the truck. With one more bump, the doors to the truck flew open and the trunk fell off the back, onto the street below. Sparks began to fly as it—and Tigger, Piglet, and Eeyore—were dragged along like a sled.

Inside her trunk, which had managed to stay open, Madeline thought she heard something. "Did you hear that?" she asked Pooh.

Pooh looked up from his now empty jar of honey. “I can hear my tummy rumbling, that’s for sure,” he answered.

Madeline shrugged. *Must have been something outside,* she thought. Whatever it was, it didn’t matter—as long as they got to her father in time to help rescue him from the Woozle. Or rather, *Winslow.*

CHAPTER FOURTEEN

Inside the Efficiency Department of Winslow Luggage, meanwhile, Christopher Robin was in desperate need of saving.

He had arrived in the lobby of the building with only minutes to spare, disheveled and feeling completely unprepared. Racing to catch the elevator just as the doors began to slide shut, he found himself alone with Giles Winslow. The man's face had a healthy glow, and he was holding a golf bag. Seeing Christopher, he shifted awkwardly on his feet. "Ready for the presentation, Robin?" he asked.

Christopher tapped the briefcase. "It's all in here," he said, nodding. Then his eyes narrowed at the clubs. "Have you been golfing?"

"Me? What? No!" Giles stammered. He pointed at

the bag. "These are . . . an area we're branching into. Golf bags. Been testing them this weekend." The elevator arrived at their floor. As the door slid open, Giles slithered out. "Right, well, see you on the dance floor. We're all counting on you." Then, before Christopher could blink, Giles slipped down the hall and into his office.

Christopher watched him go, trying to tamp down the anger he felt boiling up inside him. Golf bags? Right. That was a whole lot of hogwash—and they both knew it. While he wanted to storm into Giles's office and give him a piece of his mind, he didn't have the time. Looking over at the clock on the wall, he realized he didn't have any time, period! He needed to get to the conference room now. The meeting was scheduled to start in less than a minute.

Racing down the hall, Christopher flung open the conference room doors and took one of the few remaining seats. The others were occupied by the members of the board, who had gathered to hear how the company was going to cut 20 percent of its operating costs. A moment later the doors swung open and Giles entered. He glanced around the table, but upon seeing that the only open seat was by Christopher, he visibly cringed. Walking over, he sat down just as his father entered the room. Everyone else stood.

"As you were," the older Winslow said, gesturing for everyone to sit.

When everyone was once again seated, Giles began to speak. "Right, well, we all know why we're here. No one wants to see the Winslow Luggage ship sink." There were murmurs of agreement from around the room. "So, hard decisions must be made. Now Robin and I worked tirelessly the whole weekend on this." He coughed awkwardly as Christopher glared at him. He went on. "But I don't want to take *all* the credit. I'll let Christopher present our solutions."

Getting to his feet, Christopher slowly headed toward the front of the table. He clutched his briefcase as though it could offer comfort. As he passed by the conference room doors, he saw his team gathered outside. They all wore identical looks of anticipation—and fear. He nodded at them, hoping to silently reassure them. Then he turned back to the room.

"Right," he began. "The good news is I've found some cuts. There's a chance the company can be saved." The board members all nodded their heads approvingly. "But it won't be easy. We need to cut overheads, find cheaper suppliers, and there are a lot of sacrifices to be made in terms of our workforce."

Outside the conference room, Macmillan, Hastings, and the others exchanged nervous glances. Sacrifices to the workforce did *not* sound promising. While they knew Christopher had their backs, they were efficiency experts. They also knew that he was going to have to do what he was going to have to do. Turning back to the conference room, they continued to listen in.

"Sacrifices are fine," Giles said. "Just show us the proposals."

Christopher bit his tongue. Sacrifices were *not* fine. But he had no choice. Giles was the boss. "It's all laid out here in my papers," he said, lifting his briefcase and placing it on the large conference table. "They are very detailed, so hold tight. . . ." His voice trailed off as the lid to the briefcase popped open, revealing . . . *nothing*!

His big folder was gone.

In its place was a collection of objects from the Hundred-Acre Wood: Pooh Sticks, haycorns, a jar of honey. As Christopher frantically rustled through them, looking for the papers, he also found a weather vane and Eeyore's tail. His mouth dropped open and his throat went dry. He stopped searching and just stared down at the briefcase.

Outside the conference room, Christopher's team watched their leader's face go pale. "He's frozen," Butterworth observed.

"Like a rabbit in the headlights," Leadbetter added.

Gallsworthy, always ready to see the negative, let out a groan. "We're all doomed!" Then he lowered his head into his hands, unwilling to watch what was going to happen next.

Back in the conference room, it wasn't pretty.

Giles was staring at Christopher, arms crossed and eyes narrowed. The board members were staring at Christopher—arms crossed and eyes narrowed. And worse still, the older Winslow was staring at Christopher, arms crossed and eyes narrowed.

"Robin," Mr. Winslow finally said, "if we don't solve this issue, we'll have no choice but to shut down. What have you got?"

Christopher looked up. He didn't know what to say. He couldn't show him—and everyone else—the collection of objects. And his mind had gone completely blank. He couldn't remember a single number he had written. He couldn't recall one of the solutions he had come up with. All he could see was haycorns. "I, uh . . ."

The clock on the wall ticked, ticked, ticked. The seconds felt like hours. Just when Christopher thought he was going to have a breakdown, his assistant burst into the conference room. Racing over, she whispered something in his ear and then pointed to the door. Evelyn stood there, her face as pale as Christopher's.

"Gentlemen," Christopher said, looking back at the table. "I have to step out for a moment. My apologies."

"What the devil are you doing?" Giles said, pushing back from the table angrily. "If you walk out that door, don't bother coming back!"

Christopher didn't even offer a response. Instead, he raced out to find out exactly what was going on. Because if Evelyn was here—and not out in the country—it couldn't be anything good.

* * *

Christopher had been right: it wasn't anything good.

Evelyn quickly filled him in. Somehow, after he had left the country house, Madeline had slipped away. Evelyn had managed to track her down to the train station, and after speaking to the ticket seller, figured out that she had gotten a train ticket to London. Unfortunately, Evelyn told Christopher, she had missed the train Madeline was on and had to race and get their car to make the drive into the city.

"Where is she?" Christopher asked, scanning the sidewalks from the passenger side of the car as it rushed around London.

"I don't know," Evelyn answered, her voice raw with emotion. "Somewhere between here and the station. She's all alone." Her voice cracked as she was overcome with guilt. This was all her fault. If she hadn't been so caught up in being mad at Christopher, she might have noticed that Madeline had slipped off. Shoving her hand into her pocket, she pulled out the note Madeline had left and handed it to her husband.

Scanning it quickly, Christopher's eyes landed on the word *expotition*. His expression grew serious. "She's not alone," he said.

"Who's she with?" Evelyn asked, taking her eyes off the road long enough to give her husband a curious look. She had been panicking ever since the moment she had found Madeline's note. Christopher, on the other hand, now seemed oddly calm. True, his face had grown a bit paler and—as she watched—he fidgeted in his seat. Evelyn knew that look, and that motion. She had seen both many times over the course of their marriage. It meant Christopher had something to tell her but wasn't sure just how to do it. She raised an eyebrow and waited for him to start talking. Because that, she also knew, was always what happened next.

Sure enough, Christopher began to talk.

At first, Evelyn wished he hadn't. Because initially, it seemed like her husband had lost his mind. Apparently, as he told it, Christopher's childhood stuffed bear, Winnie the Pooh, had found him in London and brought him back—through a green door in a tree—to a place called the Hundred-Acre Wood, to help rescue the rest of his childhood friends. But as Christopher went on with his story, something happened. It was as though a light that had been off inside of him had suddenly switched back on. Her husband's eyes grew brighter; his voice grew lighter.

And by the time Christopher began to tell her about his other friends, which, if she were to believe him, included a talking piglet, owl, rabbit, kangaroo (and her baby), and "Tigger," whatever that was, Christopher's mouth, which Evelyn had been convinced was stuck in a perpetual frown, had started to lift at the corners. And she, to her shock, had started to go along with his story.

"What's a Tigger?" she heard herself ask when Christopher mentioned a creature she had never heard of before.

"Tiggers?" Christopher said, growing more animated. He hadn't realized how much he had wanted to tell Evelyn everything until he started. Now he didn't want to stop. He failed, unfortunately, to comprehend her still outwardly disbelieving expression. So he went on. "Well, they're wonderful things. Their tops are made out of rubber, their bottoms are made out of springs."

The description complete, he continued his tale. "Anyway, I pretended there was a Heffalump. But there wasn't really a Heffalump."

Reality crashed over Evelyn. She had let Christopher tell his tall tale because it had felt nice to have him share with her and she had loved seeing him smile. But a "Heffalump"? And an animal made out of rubber? She had to put a stop to this before it went too far. "Are you hearing yourself?" Evelyn asked, cutting him off. "You need to quit."

Christopher shrugged. "I think that decision's about to be made for me," he said. Then, out of the corner of his eye, he saw a flash of orange-and-black stripes disappear around a corner up ahead. Tigger! It had to be! "There they are! Left, left!"

While Evelyn wasn't entirely sure she should listen to anything her husband had to say, she turned left. A few cars ahead of them, she saw a Winslow Luggage truck rumbling along. She narrowed her eyes. It was dragging something, but she couldn't quite make out what.

"I'm telling you, it was Tigger!" Christopher said, pointing toward the truck. "He must've been with the others."

Evelyn snapped her head toward Christopher. "Darling," she said, trying to sound calm, though she was convinced she was going to have to commit her husband after they found Madeline, "these creatures aren't real. Listen, I'll call Doctor Cunningham on Monday. I think with some rest and—"

WHUMP!

The car shook as something hit the windshield.

WHUMP! WHUMP!

Evelyn's head snapped back toward the windshield. Then her mouth fell open. There, squished up against the pane of glass, were a donkey, a pig, and what could only be a Tigger!

"Hey, Christopher Robin!" Tigger said, smiling at his friend. On the far side of the car, the now empty trunk, which Tigger had managed to free them from right before it broke loose from the truck, bounced a few feet before smashing into the curb. Tigger started to tell Christopher what he had done, but before he could, Piglet spoke.

"You must be Christopher Robin's wife," he said to Evelyn. "How do you do?"

Evelyn's mouth opened and closed like a fish out of water, gasping for air. Then she looked over at Christopher. He hadn't been making up stories. He wasn't going crazy. Somehow, these animals were real. They were real *and* they were the only link she had to her daughter. Pulling the car over, she had Christopher quickly bring them inside the vehicle.

"Where's Madeline?" Christopher asked as the three got settled on the seat.

"In a truck headed W-w-w-woozle-wards!" Piglet answered.

Christopher and Evelyn exchanged a shared glance with one another. Then Evelyn put her foot to the pedal and pushed down—hard. Wrenching the wheel, she steered the car back into traffic and once again headed toward the Winslow Luggage building, right where they believed the truck they were now pursuing was headed.

Chapter Fifteen

Madeline looked up at the big stone building in front of her. She and Pooh had made it! The truck had stopped in front just as Madeline had hoped, and she and the bear had managed to sneak out before anyone could spot them. She needed to get inside and find her father. But when she glanced up at the large clock on the top of the building, she frowned. It was after eleven. They were late. And they didn't have her father's papers.

"Oh, look!" Pooh cried. Madeline turned her head just in time to see Pooh pick a pile of papers off the top of a trash pile on the street corner. "It's the Important Papers."

Not sure how they got there, but not concerned, Madeline grabbed them out of his outstretched hand

and smiled. Late or not, they had to get these to her father. Quickly, Madeline grabbed Pooh with her free hand and marched toward the entrance to the building. "We did it, Pooh!" she said, smiling down at the bear.

Pooh smiled back. "We've saved Christopher Robin!"

But just as the words left his mouth, a strong gust of wind blew down the city street. Madeline let out a cry as the gust threw her off-balance. Flinging her hands in the air, she sent Pooh—and the Important Papers—flying. Instantly, the light sheets were picked up by the wind and carried up, up, and away. "No!" Madeline shouted, trying to grab a sheet but missing. She reached for another, but again she couldn't clutch it. Over and over she tried to save the papers, and over and over again, she failed. All she had, when the wind died down, was half a sheet that she had ripped right before it, too, got swept away.

Madeline sunk to the ground, her eyes filling with tears. In the sky above, the papers floated farther and farther away from her. "No, no, no, no," Madeline said.

She had failed. And now she was going to end up going to boarding school.

"Christopher Robin!"

Pooh's excited shout made Madeline look up. To her surprise, she saw her father running toward her. "Daddy!" she said, getting to her feet.

"Thank God I found you," he said, reaching her and pulling her into a tight hug. Behind him was her mom, helping the others out of the car. Evelyn waited, letting father and daughter have their moment.

"I'm so glad a Woozle didn't eat you," Pooh said when Christopher finally stopped hugging his daughter.

Christopher smiled down at the bear. "So am I," he said. Then he turned back to Madeline. Before he could utter a syllable, the little girl began to cry.

"I lost your papers," she said. "I'm so sorry."

Squatting down, he gently put his hands on her shoulders. "Oh, Madeline," he said, his voice soft and full of love, "that really doesn't matter."

"But your work is so important," Madeline said. "I

thought that maybe if I brought you your papers you wouldn't send me away, and we could all be together. Look, I saved a little bit." She held out the small ripped piece of paper.

For a moment, Christopher was speechless. Her response broke his heart. Wiping away a tear, he gave Madeline another hug. Then, looking her right in the eye, he spoke. "Thank you for trying, my darling. And I'm sorry. Sorry for being a Father of Very Little Brain." He paused, wanting the next words to sink in, wishing that once upon a time, his own father could have said the same thing. "Of course you don't have to go away."

Madeline flung her arms around her father's neck. Her smile stretched from ear to ear as Christopher hugged her back. It was the biggest and best and warmest hug of her life.

"I can read you a bedtime story every night," Christopher whispered into her ear.

"I'd like that," Madeline whispered back.

"You gave us a real fright."

Christopher and Madeline pulled apart at the sound

of Evelyn's voice. Turning, they saw her standing a few feet away, a tearful smile on her face. Then she made her way to them and flung her arms around them both. The family stood, reunited, as the Hundred-Acre Wood gang watched, happy to see them all together.

"Well, another disastrous expotition," Eeyore said, looking on. While his voice was droll, his eyes were warm. Even he, the grumpiest of grumps, was touched by the scene unfolding in front of them.

Hearing him, Evelyn disengaged herself from the hug. She couldn't remember the last time Christopher had hugged either of them so strongly and with such intensity. She still wasn't quite sure how any of this was possible, but if these animals had helped him find his humanity, she owed them—a lot. "Oh, I don't know, Eeyore," she finally said, smiling at the dour donkey. "It all depends on how you look at things."

It all depends on how you look at things. Evelyn's words bounced around Christopher's head. His brain twitched and itched as an idea formed. He had spent so long looking at the numbers with just one thought in mind—cutting cost. What if, he suddenly realized as the idea took shape, he looked at the numbers a different way? He glanced down at the single piece of ripped paper in his hands.

Christopher smiled.

He—or rather Evelyn—had just saved his job. And possibly the company. Planting a surprising kiss on his wife's cheek, he turned and ran toward the lobby. Behind him, Evelyn and Madeline grabbed the animals and followed.

* * *

A few moments later, Christopher barged into the conference room. His family stayed right outside. In their arms, the animals "played nap time," but they didn't play it well. They were too excited to see the Woozle.

"Stop!" Christopher shouted, startling Mr. Winslow, his son, Giles, and the board members. "I have the answer!"

Mr. Winslow raised one grey eyebrow. He had spent the better part of the past hour listening to his wretch of a son lie through his teeth about working, when he knew Giles had spent the weekend golfing. He had spent another part of that hour trying to explain to the board members why they shouldn't immediately fire Christopher, despite his erratic behavior. And then, just as he had managed to convince them, Christopher had come barreling back in with a crazed look in his eye. "This better be worth the wait," Winslow said when Christopher had caught his breath.

"Oh, it is," Christopher said, nodding emphatically. "Because the answer to all your problems is . . ." He paused, letting the suspense build. "Nothing."

"Nothing?" Mr. Winslow repeated.

"Nothing comes from nothing, Robin," Giles said, not bothering to hide the smirk on his face.

But Christopher went on. "That's where you're wrong," he said. "Doing Nothing leads to the very best Something." As he spoke, he looked toward the door, where Evelyn stood with Pooh in her arms. He smiled at Pooh. The bear was smiling back proudly. Walking over to the overhead projector, Christopher placed the piece of ripped paper on it. "What happens when people have time off from work? Nothing to do?" he asked the room.

His query was answered with silence. The board members stared back at him blankly.

"They go on holiday," Christopher said, answering his own question. "And what do people need to go on holiday?"

Once more, he was met with silence.

"Luggage," he said, answering his own question—again. He turned to his boss. "Mr. Winslow, you employ thousands of people across all your companies. If you gave them all paid holidays—"

"*Paid* holidays?" Mr. Winslow repeated, beginning to think Giles had been right about Christopher's mental stability—or lack thereof. The board seemed to be thinking the same thing. The room filled with their disbelieving laughter.

Christopher was not swayed. He switched the projector on, and a graph of Winslow's wealthiest customers filled the wall. He went to point at it but realized he didn't have a pointer. Scanning the desk, his eyes landed on his open briefcase. Grabbing a Pooh Stick, he continued. "At the moment, you're only selling to the wealthy and no one else. But look . . ." He pointed at the graph with the Pooh Stick. "If *more of us* could afford to go on holiday, it would mean hundreds of thousands of ordinary people going off to the countryside and lakes and beaches . . . with their Winslow Luggage. And if we made our prices cheaper, *everyone* could afford to buy them." He stopped and waited.

He didn't have to wait long.

"*Great*," Giles said sarcastically. "Our lovely beaches crammed with the hoi polloi and their gramophones and bottles of cider." He winced as though the thought itself were revolting.

His father, on the other hand, was not so quick to pass judgment. He raised a hand. "Now hold on, Giles . . ."

"Oh, Father, please!" Giles snapped. "This is clearly codswallop!"

"Well, you would say that, wouldn't you, Giles?" Christopher said, jumping in between father and son.

Giles's face turned red and he angrily pushed away from the table, getting to his feet. "And why, pray tell, is that?" he asked.

Christopher ignored the threatening look Giles was giving him. Instead, he shrugged. And then, as if it were the most obvious answer in the world, he replied, "Because you are a Woozle!"

In the doorway, Pooh perked up, forgetting for a moment to play nap time. "So that's what a Woozle looks like," he said, pleased to have finally seen one. The Woozle was definitely as scary as he had imagined it would be—right down to its mean, beady eyes.

"And what the devil is a Woozle?" Giles asked.

"A Woozle," Christopher answered, "is a slinking little monster who gets everyone to do his work for him and hopes we forget what's really important in our lives: our families, our dear old friends, the people who love us, the people we love." As he spoke, he walked over to the door. Gesturing to Evelyn, Madeline, and his team, which had gathered to see what would happen, he brought them into the conference room. Then he put one arm around Evelyn—and one around Katherine. "Well," he went on, "I'm here to tell you that we're not afraid of Heffalumps and Woozles anymore!"

Giles looked back and forth between Christopher, his father, and the gathered onlookers. Then he shook his head. "Good Lord, he's lost his marbles!"

"Has he?"

Mr. Winslow's response surprised not only Giles, but Christopher as well. Both men turned and looked over at the business owner curiously.

"Let's address the Heffalump in the room, shall we?" Mr. Winslow went on, looking at his son pointedly. "What were you doing this weekend, Giles?"

Giles fidgeted nervously. He gulped and pulled at his necktie. "Me?" he asked, trying to sound innocent. "I told you, I . . . I was working." As a bead of sweat began to roll down his temple, Giles reached into his pocket for a handkerchief. Instead, he pulled out a golf ball.

Mr. Winslow's brow furrowed. "What on? Your golf

swing?" he asked. His expression grew disappointed and he shook his head. "I've not heard of a Woozle before, son, but from the sound of it . . . you are one."

"Me? A Woozle? But—" Giles stammered.

"Sit down, Giles!" Mr. Winslow ordered. Then he turned and looked over at Christopher, who still stood in front of the door. "Congratulations, Robin. I'd like you to start on this immediately." The others let out cheers and even the board members, who had been watching everything with a mixture of confusion and fascination, began to applaud.

Smiling from ear to ear, Christopher took Mr. Winslow's outstretched hand and shook it. "Thank you, sir," he said sincerely. Then he glanced over his shoulder at Evelyn and Madeline. "But I'm going to do Nothing for a while myself now."

Mr. Winslow nodded. "Because when you do Nothing, it leads to the very best of a Something," he said, repeating Christopher's words back to him. "Did I get that right?"

"Close enough, sir," Christopher said. "Close enough."

Then, turning, he took his family's hands in his and walked out of the boardroom. Over his shoulder, he heard Giles let out a squeak. "That bear was staring at me!" the man said.

"A bear, staring at you?" Mr. Winslow said. "Clearly, you've gone crackers."

Looking down at Pooh, who was now flopped over Madeline's shoulder, Christopher saw that the bear was still playing nap time. But sensing Christopher's gaze, Pooh lifted his head ever so slightly. Then he smiled. Christopher smiled back. "Silly old bear," he mouthed.

But Christopher was only teasing. Pooh wasn't silly. He wasn't silly at all. He was the best bear in the whole wide world. And Christopher couldn't wait to get back to the Hundred-Acre Wood with Pooh and practice doing Nothing. After all, he had wasted too much time already doing too much of Everything.

EPILOGUE

"SOMETIMES THE SMALLEST THINGS
TAKE UP THE MOST ROOM IN YOUR HEART."
—WINNIE THE POOH

"Oh, boy, it's good to be home."

Walking through the green door and into the sunshine of the Hundred-Acre Wood, Christopher had to agree with Piglet. He took a deep breath, inhaling the air that now smelled sweeter and squinting under a sun that felt warmer somehow. Behind him, he heard the door creak farther open and turned in time to see Evelyn and Madeline appear.

As they straightened up and began to look around at the Hundred-Acre Wood for the first time, Christopher just watched. The smile on his face grew broader as Madeline let out a happy little squeal and began to skip after Pooh, Piglet, Tigger, and Eeyore. Her eyes were bright and her shoulders light. She was, finally, enjoying being a child. Reaching over, he took Evelyn's hand in his and squeezed. Then they, too, began to follow the others.

While they walked, Christopher pointed out the sights of the wood. Passing Pooh Sticks Bridge, he told Evelyn and Madeline all about the game of Pooh Sticks. When they walked by Owl's house—now safely back in the tree—Christopher told them all about defeating the Heffalump. With every adventure he recalled, Christopher felt the years fall away. Through the eyes of his wife and daughter, he was getting to experience the Hundred-Acre Wood like it was when he was a child.

Finally, they reached the picnic spot where all important events in the wood were held. Rabbit, Owl, Kanga, and Roo were waiting. Over the table, a banner was hanging that read: WELCOM ROBIN FAMILY. Seeing the spelling error, Evelyn turned and raised an amused eyebrow at Christopher. *Expotition*, she mouthed, just before being swallowed up in a hug from Kanga.

Noting the sign and listening to the others welcome everyone back, Eeyore nodded slowly. "On the happiest day of the year," he said gloomily. "My birthday."

"Today?" Roo asked at the same time as Piglet said, "Your birthday?"

"No presents and no proper notice taken of me at all," Eeyore said in answer. "Everything is back to normal."

Listening to his old friend, Christopher bit his cheek and tried not to smile. Everything *was* back to normal—finally. And it felt wonderful. Then he cocked his head. Well, not quite *everything*. Reaching into his pocket, he pulled out Eeyore's tail. He walked over and pinned it on the morose donkey. "*Now* everything is back to normal," he said.

As the others laughed and began to enjoy the picnic, Christopher's eyes scanned the clearing. Pooh was missing the festivities. Whispering in Evelyn's ear that he would be right back, Christopher left the party—but not before grabbing a jar of honey.

As he walked away from the picnic area, he could hear Madeline's sweet and happy laugh followed by a chuckle from Evelyn. He wondered why he had spent so long trying to keep this place hidden from them—and from himself. With all the bad things he had seen, with all the troubles he had had to deal with, the Hundred-Acre Wood and his friends were like a healing balm. He never should have left. And as he went to find Pooh, he vowed silently that he would *never* keep his daughter from this place. He would let her enjoy life and the innocence that the wood brought for as long as he could. It was the least he could do.

But first, he needed to find Pooh. And he had a pretty good idea where his friend had gone.

Making his way quickly through the woods, Christopher crested the small hill that led to the Enchanted Spot. Sure enough, Pooh was already there, sitting on the log. Walking over, Christopher sat down and then handed Pooh the jar of honey.

Delighted by the snack (after all, Pooh was hungry—again), the bear dug in immediately. For a while, they just sat there, content to be doing absolutely Nothing. Finally, Pooh looked up from his honey. His nose was covered in the sticky sweetness and his paw was dripping. "Christopher Robin," he asked, "what day is it?"

Christopher smiled at the bear. He knew this refrain. They had had this exact conversation hundreds of times before. Still, he played along happily. "It's Today," he answered.

"My favorite day," Pooh said with a nod.

"Mine too, Pooh," Christopher agreed. "Mine too."

Pooh looked thoughtful for a moment. Then he spoke again. "Yesterday, when it was Tomorrow, was too exciting a day for me," he said, surprising Christopher. This was *not* part of their usual banter.

But Christopher had to agree. Yesterday had been too exciting. Yet, he wouldn't have traded it for the world. For without yesterday, today wouldn't be happening. And without yesterday—or any of the days before, for that matter—Christopher wouldn't have been able to understand how truly special this moment was, or how lucky he was now. "Silly old bear," Christopher finally said. Then, putting his arm over his friend's soft and furry shoulders, Christopher turned and looked out at the sun as it once again began to sink behind the horizon of the Hundred-Acre Wood. Beside him, Pooh did the same.

And that is how they stayed as the sun sank lower and lower. Two friends, reunited, happily doing . . . Nothing.